MY DINNER *with* ANDREW

TOUCHED
BY AN
ANGEL

MY DINNER *with* ANDREW

Story and teleplay by
MARTHA WILLIAMSON,
EXECUTIVE PRODUCER

Novelization by
ROBERT TINE

Based on the television series created by
JOHN MASIUS

THOMAS NELSON PUBLISHERS
Nashville

Published in Nashville, Tennessee, by Thomas Nelson, Inc.

Baby in the closet allegory courtesy of C. S. Lewis.

Library of Congress Cataloging-in-Publication Data
Tine, Robert.

My dinner with Andrew / story and teleplay by Martha Williamson, executive producer; novelization [i.e., novelization] by Robert Tine; based on the television series by John Masius.

    p.   cm.

Based on a script from the TV series *Touched By An Angel.*
ISBN 0-7852-7130-9 (pbk.)

1. Masius, John. II. Williamson, Martha. My dinner with Andrew. III. Touched by an angel (Television program) IV. Title.
PS3570.I48M9 1998
813'.54—dc21

98–19479
CIP

Printed in the United States of America
1 2 3 4 5 6 7 QBK 03 02 01 00 99 98

Chapter One

$\mathscr{M}$onica had been standing alone for hours in the opulent lobby of the Park Place Palace Hotel, which was not the most comfortable place to be. With the passing of every minute she felt more and more out of place there in the lobby of what was perhaps New York's most exclusive and luxurious hotel.

It was just before lunchtime, and the lobby was crowded with travelers coming and going, checking in and checking out. In the midst of it all, Monica couldn't help but notice the large contingent of New Yorkers known as "ladies who lunch." The hotel was playing host to some kind of charity function, and nothing brought out the ladies who lunch like a good, fashionable cause.

Most of these women were rich—either in their own right through inheritance and long generations of old family money or, as the "old" fortunes died out, through the more common path of fortuitous marriage to wealthy men who made their money themselves, for the most part on Wall Street or in New York's exceptionally rich real estate market. And wealth conveyed instant prestige in a money-conscious place like Manhattan.

The ladies who married their money were often different from those who had the good fortune to inherit. For one thing, the ladies who possessed the newer fortunes tended to be social in the extreme. At the beginning of the New York "season," which ran from the early fall through Christmas and into the late spring, a certain segment of New York society knew, well in advance, the social events they would be attending over the course of the next four or five months.

There were small luncheons and grand affairs, antique shows and masked balls, dinners and dances and museum benefits, auctions, receptions, book parties, galas, and other glittering events punctuating the cold winter months. Some events were more prestigious than others, and, of those, some towered over the season. The Winter Antiques Show, the Gala at the Metropolitan Museum of Art Costume Collection, and Tables of Contents for the New York Public Library were very hot tickets. Being seen at these events was mandatory for everyone who was anyone— or who aspired to be someone in the rarefied air of New York City society.

The social season coincided with the opera season, and whether one cared for music or not, everyone was expected to attend Alice Tully Hall at least three or four times during the season, much as one might have in the days of old New York. The ballet was on at the same time as well, so the social set spent a number of nights with the American Ballet Theater, again, whether they liked it or not. Certain Broadway shows were must-sees, but tickets were bought six months in advance to every new opening of the season. Who knew in March what the hot ticket would be in October?

For the most part, the ladies who lunch were accompanied by their rich husbands if an activity was set for the evening. By day, their husbands went to keep up the family fortune, and the ladies and their special luncheons held the social field alone.

Then, suddenly, it would all come to an abrupt end.

By Memorial Day, at the absolute latest, the season in New York was over, and the ladies who lunch would have moved their whole lives to summer places like the Hamptons, discreet estates in the Hudson Valley, exclusive islands in the Caribbean, and to a couple of select spots in Europe. But by summer's end they were ready to return to Manhattan and do it all over again.

Oddly enough, for ladies who lunch, food was the least important element of the lunch itself. The social interaction was the most meaningful component of a charity luncheon, an exchange of intelligence important in society: gossip, of course—who was dating whom, or who was wearing which designer. Since everybody already knew which restaurants, clubs, and designers were in vogue that season, the most vital piece of information one could glean at a luncheon of this sort was the name of the *next* big thing. The next place to be seen, the next designer to be seen wearing—essential information, as anyone can see.

The lunch itself was never much. A mesclun salad, a small piece of lightly grilled fish, a dab of green vegetable (preferably an exotic one— bitter broccoli rabe was the veggie of the moment), a sip of mineral water, and a thimble-size cup of espresso were about the most any one of them would consume.

And while this all might sound shallow and vacuous, it served a very important function.

The ladies who lunch were also passionately dedicated to a number of charities—the *right* charities, of course. And despite leading what many people considered superficial and rather frivolous lives, these ladies still managed to accomplish a great deal of good. A pack of ladies who lunch in full charity gallop could raise millions of dollars for a variety of good causes. Monica reflected on all this while she waited, telling herself that

God could bring something good from the strangest of sources.

All the women in the room were dressed to the nines, in clothes that were the last word in the latest fashion, couture that cost in the thousands. Needless to say, Monica felt that she stood out for being underdressed in her simple white shirt and khaki slacks. Her discomfort was further compounded by the fact that she had absolutely no idea why she was there in the first place.

So she stood there, feeling ever more self-conscious, taking in the action around her, rocking from heel to toe, wondering why she had been called to that place at that time and trying to look as inconspicuous as possible in such a sophisticated crowd. She need not have worried, of course—none of the ladies who lunch even noticed her. She was far and away, down beneath their supremely sensitive social radar.

Monica scanned the room one more time and finally found, to her immense surprise, a friendly face. She felt a warm feeling of relief wash over her and she smiled brightly, threading her way through the crowd to reach her newfound friend.

Monica's friend was not one of the ladies, though. Rather it was a bird, a gorgeously colored parrot sitting on his perch in the middle of the lobby, watching the hubbub with much the same apprehension that Monica had. He looked as if he, too, would rather be elsewhere.

"Hello," Monica whispered gently, keeping her voice low so as not to startle the beautiful bird. "I must say, you're looking very lovely today." She glanced around the room. "It's nice to see somebody else who's wondering what he's doing in a place like this . . ."

The parrot looked at Monica with something approaching comprehension, as if he understood that the two of them just did not belong there. He raised his beautiful red and green wings slightly, shrugging as if saying, "What are you gonna do?"

"How lovely you are, though," Monica continued. "Such beautiful plumage . . ."

Monica had not noticed that Tess had made her way through the throng and was now standing directly behind her, looking highly amused as Monica continued to rattle on to the parrot.

"It's rather a tony crowd, don't you think? And so well dressed—it's like a fashion show, isn't it? I feel a little underdressed, actually. You sir, however, you put the whole lot of them to shame in those lovely feathers of yours. How long have you been here at this very grand hotel, if you don't mind my asking?"

Tess heard the question and could not resist. She leaned in close to Monica's ear.

"Five years!" she chirped.

Monica yelped and jumped as if she had been pinched, then whirled around to find Tess. Her supervisor was smiling broadly, vastly amused by the trick she had played on the unsuspecting angel.

"Oh, Tess!" cried Monica. "You frightened me half to death. I think my heart stopped beating for a second."

"Sorry, baby," said Tess, laughing out loud. "When I saw you yakking away to that bird I just couldn't resist. You'd have done it yourself if you'd caught me."

"Very funny," Monica grumbled, feeling her own feathers ruffled by Tess' little prank. "Though I doubt I'd actually dare."

Tess continued to laugh heartily. "Oh, baby, if you could only get a look at your face!"

Monica stood her ground. "Well," she said sternly, "you'd start talking to birds, too, if you'd spent hours standing around here. I thought I'd go mad having to wait for so long."

Tess stopped laughing, and she frowned slightly. "Hours?" she said. "You've been here that long already? Where is Andrew?" There was a little growl in Tess' voice, a sound that the angels under her supervision had come to know and dread.

"Andrew?" Monica replied. "I don't know where he is. I guess I thought he would be with you. And while we're on the subject, what *are* we doing here anyway, Tess?"

Tess shook her head slowly. "I wish I knew. Oh, I do not like these last-minute things. I do not," she said emphatically. "There's no time to do your homework. Shooting from the hip like this . . . something's always bound to fall through the cracks."

Monica nodded. It was no secret that Tess ran a very tight ship. But both Monica, the case-worker, and Tess, her supervisor, knew that as angels they were required to work on a need-to-know basis. It had always been that way. Angels don't know everything . . . but God does.

Tess turned and looked at the crowd. She looked less than impressed with what she saw. The fashionable ladies were everywhere, chatting, twittering like flocks of well-dressed birds, no one paying the slightest bit of attention to Tess and Monica. Not one of those women was aware that they were in the presence of two extraordinary creatures. While Tess looked older than Monica, she gave no indication of just how *ancient* she really was.

Tess had been sent by God to earth thousands of years before. Her first assignment on earth had been in ancient Rome. She had been a minor functionary in the royal palace of Augustus Caesar, an official who just happened to have been set down in the very heart of the known world. Tess had been the emperor's food taster—an important but dangerous post. The Romans of that era had a genuine knack for the use of poisons, and it was one of the most popular ways of doing away with unpopular emperors. Fortunately, she had never taken a dose of poison for her employer—Augustus had been nothing less than beloved of his subjects.

In the succeeding centuries she had worked all over the world and had encountered all kinds of people. Tess had met the famous and the lowly, the saintly and the direst of sinners. She had done God's work tirelessly and had known inspiring triumphs and heartbreaking defeats when humans would not open their hearts to hear the message of God. She took no pride in her successes, just as she refused to carry the burden of those moments of defeat. God's work went on, and she trusted that His words would never return void without accomplishing what they were sent out to do.

It had taken a while for the two angels to actually meet. Tess and Monica didn't become a team until 1,939 years after Tess' arrival in ancient Rome. They met a long way from Rome too—in rural New Jersey, on the night when Orson Welles from the Mercury Theater was

11

scaring the daylights out of the entire country with his radio broadcast *War of the Worlds.*

That first encounter between Monica and Tess was not a pleasant one. Tess had been forced to reprimand Monica after she had added to the panic of the night by making an annunciation to an already spooked bunch of people. It was then that Monica learned a valuable lesson: Timing is everything.

The unfortunate first meeting between Tess and Monica was all in the very distant past now, and the two of them worked well together—despite Tess' penchant for practical jokes. Although there were times when Tess lost patience with Monica, she cared for her charges deeply and was proud of the progress Monica had made over the years.

Monica scanned the crowd and this time— and with some relief—saw someone she knew. Andrew was making his way toward them almost at a run, as if he were in a terrific hurry.

"There he is!" said Monica, pointing at Andrew.

"And doesn't he look nice?" said Tess.

In contrast to Tess and Monica, Andrew *did*

look as if he belonged in the luxurious lobby of the Park Place Palace Hotel. He was dressed in a faultlessly fitted, dove gray, double-breasted suit and a crisp white shirt. At his throat was a perfectly knotted, tasteful silk tie.

"Hi," said Andrew, walking up to them. "I finally made it. I was worried there for a moment. I got the call to be here at the very last minute."

Tess looked him over from head to toe like a sergeant examining a soldier on a parade ground.

"Well," she said slowly, "whatever it is, whatever's going on here, you certainly dressed for it."

"Thanks," said Andrew. He looked from Monica to Tess. "So what is it? What is this all about?"

"What is what?" Tess demanded.

A slight look of puzzlement appeared on Andrew's face. "The assignment, Tess. What is it?"

Tess threw her hands up in disgust. "You don't know? Doesn't anyone know? Oh, for heaven's sake."

Monica was as puzzled as the other two angels. "What is happening here?"

13

But Andrew was clueless. "I don't know. Is something going on, or did we get called here for no good reason?"

The frustration in Tess' voice was plain to hear. "I got word that *you* needed help, Andrew," she told him. "And you needed it in a great big hurry, too."

Monica nodded. "So did I."

Although primarily an Angel of Death, Andrew often assisted Monica and Tess with their assignments. He could, however, revert to his official capacity at any time (even if he was in the middle of working on a case with Tess and Monica).

Andrew shrugged. "I don't need any help. I mean, not that I know of. I just got a message to show up here and wait. I figured it was going to be something sudden—a heart attack or something like that."

He looked around the crowded room, puzzlement still showing on his face. "It's funny, though," he added. "I usually know at least *something* about the case beforehand."

Tess shook her head and looked disgusted. "See what I mean, Miss Wings?" she said to

Monica. "Just what I was saying a minute ago—
when you shoot from the hip, something is going
to slip through the—"

"*You!*" The word came from across the room
and was loud enough to cut through the general noise in the room.

Tess, Monica, and Andrew turned to see a
woman bearing down on them. She could have
been the prototype of a lady who lunches. She was
dressed as lunching lady par excellence, clad in a
stunning piece of Chanel couture that was part
of the uniform of the upper echelon of this already
elite group. Her blonde hair was perfectly coiffed,
her nails and makeup looked as if they had been
applied by professionals.

In addition, there was a no-nonsense atti-
tude about the woman, a sense that she was quite
comfortable issuing orders and had no conception that they might not be obeyed instantly. It
was plain that she exuded that air of command
shared by very rich women and very high-rank-
ing military officers.

"You!" she repeated, plucking at Andrew's
sleeve. She paid not the slightest attention to either

Monica or Tess. "Well, thank goodness I've found you. You have no idea what a bind I'm in—and you are the one who is going to get me out of it."

Andrew was nonplussed by the sudden attention. "Uh, yes ma'am," he said. "Can I, uh, help you with something?"

"Besides saving my life?" the woman said. "No, that will be quite enough for one day."

Andrew smiled. "As you wish, ma'am." He was something of an expert in saving lives—though not in any way that the woman could have imagined.

She thrust out a perfectly manicured hand.

"Jackie Cysse," she said. She spoke as if those two words, that name alone, spoke volumes. When Andrew did not respond immediately she repeated her name again. "Jackie Cysse." She sounded a little on the impatient side.

"Ah . . . ," said Andrew, not quite sure what to say next. Though, somewhere in the back of his mind the name "Cysse" did sound vaguely familiar.

"I know you," Jackie Cysse said, her eyes

narrowing as she peered at Andrew. "I'm sure I do. Don't I?"

"I'm . . . not sure," Andrew replied.

"I just *know* I've seen you before," said Jackie forcefully. She gave the distinct impression that she felt she was never wrong about anything. "Did you work with my husband? Harvey Cysse. You know, as in Cysse Petroleum? You must know *that* name."

Andrew knew of the endless chain of filling stations that stretched from one coast to the other, but he was focusing on the name itself.

"Harvey . . ." He had encountered so many people, so many names during his tenure as Angel of Death that it was difficult to conjure up any specific name and face in an instant. After all, like Monica, he had been in service since 1938, and as Angel of Death he had come on just in time for the busy years of the Second World War.

"Cysse," Jackie filled in.

Then Andrew remembered.

The room in the hospital had been luxurious—more like a lavish hotel suite than anything you usually found in a hospital, but Harvey Cysse was so rich he was able to afford to die in very grand style. Then Andrew remembered Harvey Cysse himself, an elderly man—a man much older than his wife—a thin and pallid form in the hospital bed, the life slipping out of him like flowing water. There was a crowd of expensive doctors and round-the-clock nurses hovering around Harvey as he died, as if money could hold back the inevitability of death.

But Cysse had died, of course, finally going with Andrew in joy and relief. "Oh, yes!" said Andrew. "Harvey! I remember Harvey Cysse. Of course . . ."

Jackie Cysse beamed and looked triumphant. "See, I *knew* you knew him. Now let's see—don't tell me—you worked for him, right? You were one of those bright young men rising to the top of Cysse Petroleum. My husband called them 'the shooting stars.'"

Andrew shook his head slowly. "Well, not exactly. I didn't actually work *for* him. I knew him very . . . very late in his life."

"That's it! I remember now," said Jackie

jubilantly. "The hospital. You were there near the end. A doctor! I never forget a face! Never! Ask anyone." As if the matter were now well and truly settled, Jackie felt as if she had a perfect right to commandeer Andrew. She snatched Andrew by the arm and pulled him away from Monica and Tess, leading him toward the door of the grand ballroom of the hotel.

It was plain to Andrew that Mrs. Harvey Cysse had no idea who he was or what he was doing there in that hotel that day—but, for reasons of her own, she was determined to make use of him.

"Well, this is just perfect," she announced, "just perfect . . ." Jackie spread her glance over Andrew again, looking at him as if seeing him for the first time. "Now, tell me again, what did you say your name was, darling?"

Andrew had been called many things, but "darling" had not come up all that often.

Andrew was unused to such straightforward treatment; truth to tell, *he* was usually the one in control of an encounter.

"Uh—Andrew," he said, fighting to control

a nervous stammer. He could not quite think what to say, but hoped that heaven would direct his words and give him a hint as to his involvement in this bizarre situation. "A friend . . . though, not a doc—"

That was as far as he got with the truth before Jackie Cysse filled in the rest for him. "Dr. Andrew Friend!" she exclaimed. She looked him up and down again then asked, "And tell me—and make sure it's the truth—are you married, darling?"

He had never been married. His answer came easily.

"No," he said emphatically. "I am not married." Perhaps his answer was too definite, because it seemed to tell Jackie she was on the right track.

"That's good. How about a girlfriend? Anyone serious? Engaged? Going steady? Living together?"

"Ah, no," said Andrew.

"Even better. Now," she said, without missing a beat, "I guess we can assume that you don't have any strange inclinations, no weird hangups, no history of stalking, drug addiction, petty theft . . . no criminal record, right?"

It was a question not often put to an angel—

Andrew had never been called upon to answer it—and it took him by surprise.

"Uh . . . ," he said—as if he had to think about it—"No. No criminal record. And no strange inclinations . . ."

"Good," said Jackie Cysse as she walked him quickly across the room, a firm grip on his arm, much in the way a bouncer might throw out an intruder at a private party. Only Jackie seemed to be forcing him *into* a party to which he had not been invited. At least, he assumed he had not been invited to this party. He wondered if this was part of the assignment, or if he just happened to be in the wrong place at the wrong time and was now being shanghaied by this rather pushy woman.

"Where are we going?" Andrew asked.

"Dr. Friend—can I call you Andy? You are about to save my life," said Jackie, unaware of the irony of the situation.

As she dragged Andrew toward the ballroom, he could only manage a quick glance over his shoulder, a desperate look back at Tess and Monica. Those two found Andrew's predicament vastly amusing, and it was all they could do to suppress their laughter.

"That boy needs help!" said Tess with a little cackle. As if agreeing with her, the parrot gave out a little screech.

"Let's go watch the fun," said Monica.

"Why not!" said Tess. The two of them followed the hapless Andrew into the ballroom.

Chapter Two

The grand ballroom of the Park Place Palace had been extravagantly decorated with thousands of dollars worth of flowers and greenery donated by a number of extremely pricey New York florists. These florists were shrewd businesspeople who, while anxious to support a good cause, were all the while well aware that ladies who lunch were likely to spend exorbitant amounts at the right society florists for their own private affairs. Spend a few thousand dollars in good advertising while helping a worthy cause, and everybody wins.

As Jackie led Andrew into the ballroom, he was confronted with a room full of ladies who lunch. There were expensively dressed women simply *everywhere*. Some stood in small groups chatting away; others were already seated at the circular banquet tables, perched in the inevitable little chairs with the spindly gold legs; some rummaged in the "goodie bags" that were a feature of luncheons like this one. Andrew caught glimpses of the glittering tidbits. The ladies seemed to be quite pleased with the gifts from upscale cosmetics companies, exclusive chocolatiers, and with the small but expensive items like change purses, address books, and fountain pens.

"These things are such a blessing," he heard one of the women say. "They make perfect gifts for the help . . ."

Jackie Cysse, it seemed, knew everyone in attendance that afternoon. As they crossed the ballroom, she never stopped waving, blowing kisses, and calling out greetings. And Andrew could not help but notice that she never seemed to pause for a response.

"Sylvia! You look so lovely in Escada!"

"Darling, Barbara! It's been far too long." She circled her finger in the air next to her ear, which apparently was the society semaphore for "Call me on the phone."

"Claudia! Your hair! It is nothing less than exquisite—still going to Freddy, I see. He's such a dear!" Andrew had to admit he was impressed that Jackie had the ability to look at someone's hair and be able to identify the stylist.

Andrew couldn't quite keep up with Jackie, who was spraying compliments around the room as if she were wielding a machine gun loaded with a full magazine of flattery. In the far corner of the room, some ladies gathered around a desk where an author was busily autographing books. And at her side, her publisher's publicist was working a credit card machine. A poster next to the table announced that the title of the book on sale was *Women Who Run with the Bulls: The Savvy Woman's Guide to Meaningful, Long-Term Investment.*

Andrew was not familiar with the title. He was still taking all this in when Jackie turned her large blue eyes on him again. "It's the Books and Bachelors Luncheon. Again, already! Where does a year go?" Jackie asked the question, but did not wait for an answer.

"Mrs. Cysse . . . ," Andrew began uncertainly. "I'm not altogether sure that I should—"

Jackie ignored him. "You know I really can't be chairman every year. It's not fair that they ask me every year knowing that I would never turn them down. Next year, though, I'm going to be firm. This is the last, absolutely the last time."

Jackie glanced over her shoulder and caught sight of yet another old friend.

"Elaine! Gorgeous de la Renta! Oscar is such a genius. You look absolutely stunning! But then again, you *always* look stunning—one day I'll find out your secret."

Jackie turned back to Andrew again. It seemed that she had not ignored him and had heard that tone in his voice—the one that suggested he was about to back out, beg off, and get out of there as gracefully but as fast as he could.

"Anyway, Dr. Friend, I cannot thank you enough. Can you believe it? I had my bachelor all set up—Ray Hannah, the cardiologist at Lenox Hill Hospital—do you know him?"

"No," said Andrew. "In fact, I'm not a—"

"Ray is absolutely the best heart man in the

city, believe me," Jackie announced emphatically. "I had him all set up, and what happens? At the last possible minute he gets paged! That little thing goes *beep*, and off he goes to save somebody's life. And what am I supposed to do? Thank God you showed up!" She smiled beatifically. "I cannot thank you enough . . ." She paused a moment to up the charm to its highest level. Had she been of a different generation she might have batted her eyelashes. "Andy . . . ," she began with a seductive smile.

Then the coin dropped in the middle of Andrew's brain. "*Waaiit* a minute," he said, the awful truth dawning on him. "Books and *Bachelors* . . ."

Jackie nodded vigorously. "It's the League's biggest fund-raiser," she said. "You probably don't read *W*, but if you did you'd see we're in there every year. And *Town and Country* and *Avenue*. And the *New York Times* "Style" section too. But don't tell me you're a doctor and you haven't heard of the Nichols BioTech Institute."

Before Andrew could answer, Jackie waved vigorously at a woman on the other side of the room. "Rachel! Rachel! You can call off the search for eligible men—" She pointed to Andrew. "I've got one. He appeared from nowhere, like an apparition or something. A genuine lifesaver. *And* he's a doctor."

Andrew could only smile weakly. "Really, Mrs. Cysse, I have to tell you—"

"Call me Jackie!"

If Andrew's smile was weak and wan, Tess and Monica, by contrast, were smiling broadly. Led by Tess, the two of them had walked into the ballroom as if they belonged there and had positioned themselves on a small mezzanine overlooking the room. It was a good vantage point from which to view the rituals and habits of Manhattan charity society in full gallop. Tess looked around at the elegant clothes and sniffed the expensive perfume that sweetened the air. Monica seemed a little seduced by the opulence, but Tess was not.

"My, my, my, my, my," she said with a shake of her head. "Aren't they all so grand?"

In her long career, Tess had encountered vanity in all its forms—from Caesar and kings down to these society ladies who lunched. She knew it to be an empty and pointless diversion and wondered how it could not be obvious to everybody else. Human vainglory had caused so much trouble throughout history that she wondered why people even bothered with it anymore. Still, free will was free will—and humans were free to do with their lives as they saw fit.

Monica was a bit puzzled by the proceedings. She stopped a passing waiter, a weary-looking man who seemed to have had *his* fill of society banquets—even if he was getting paid for them.

"Pardon me," Monica asked, "but just what is a Books and Bachelors Luncheon?"

The waiter shrugged and smiled wryly. "They eat lunch, they buy books, they auction off men," he said. "They raise a lot of money for a good cause."

Monica gulped "They auction off men?" she said with a gasp. "What does that mean?"

"Just for the night," said the waiter as he walked on. The old man seemed quite blasé about it, but Monica was having a certain amount of trouble getting her mind around the concept. The books she could grasp; the sale of unmarried men to a group of high-society women was another thing altogether.

"Auctioning off men?" repeated Monica as she turned to Tess. "That's not legal, is it?"

Tess laughed loudly. "I'm afraid it is, Miss Wings."

"Well," said Monica, "now I've heard everything."

Tess laughed again. "Honey, you have barely begun. When you've finished your term as a caseworker, *then* you will have heard everything. Right now, you've hardly scratched the surface."

Andrew managed to break free from Jackie, and he hurried over to Tess and Monica, grateful to see two familiar faces. He looked distinctly distressed by the way events were unfolding that afternoon.

"Do you know what this is?" he asked Tess and Monica. "Have you any idea what is going to happen here?" He looked quite agitated about the predicament in which he found himself.

Andrew might have been upset by the imbroglio, but Tess was enjoying the angel's discomfort immensely.

"I know what *you* are, Bachelor Boy," she said with a huge smile on her face. "And remember, it's for a good cause. That's the important thing."

But Andrew didn't care how good the cause was. He shook his head slowly.

"No, uh-uh," he said as firmly as he could. "I am *not* doing this, Tess. I *can't* do it."

"Well, why not?" asked Tess. "Maybe it's part of the assignment. You can't miss part of the assignment."

"But what if it's not?" Andrew countered. "Tess, it's . . . humiliating." The whole thing just did not sit well with him, and Andrew was definitely *not* prepared to enter into the auction in the spirit of fun.

"Well," said Monica, joining into the spirit of the game, "Tess did say it was for a good cause. Isn't it, Tess?"

Tess nodded vigorously. "The Nichols BioTech Institute does some very fine work. And now you're part of it, Andrew."

A hangdog look came over Andrew's handsome features, and he looked down at his elegant, thin-soled shoes. "This can't be why I'm here." He sighed heavily. "How did I get into this? I cannot believe this is part of the assignment."

"I don't know," said Tess. "None of us know." She was in command now. No more joking around. "But we all got sent here, and this is what happened. There's got to be a reason for all this. So I say 'Go with the flow until you know,' baby."

Andrew looked less than convinced. "I'm not so sure that's the best thing to do, Tess."

"Do you see an alternative?" Monica asked him. "What else can you do?"

Andrew considered this for a moment. "I could . . . run away as quickly as possible," he suggested.

"Don't be silly," said Tess, laughing. "This is something you're going to have to go through. And besides—you never know. You might enjoy being in a bachelor auction."

"I'll never live it down," complained Andrew.

Tess nodded. "Now *that* is probably very true, Angel Boy. Very true indeed."

And time had run out. It was too late for any last-minute maneuvers. As Andrew stood there, Jackie Cysse descended on him and, in an instant, had him in her well-manicured clutches again.

"There you are, Andy!" she said. "Come along now. We're starting. I've put you at a table with some very, very *special* friends of mine."

"Who are they?" Andrew asked miserably.

"Oh, you'll see," Jackie answered. "You'll find out in a minute or two."

Tess and Monica waved good-bye, their amusement at Andrew's predicament showing plainly on their faces. Andrew was looking back at them, frowning with an "I'll get you for this" look on his face, as Jackie led him back through the crowd. He was not watching where he was going, and Jackie was engaged again in a round of rapid-fire meet-and-greets.

Andrew bumped squarely into a woman in the middle of the room, colliding with enough force to almost knock her down. Andrew scrambled to catch her before she toppled.

"I'm so sorry!" said Andrew. "My fault."

"That's—" She looked up into Andrew's face and for a moment could not speak. Andrew looked so familiar . . . yet she knew that she had never seen him before in her life.

The woman Andrew had bumped into was dressed in a simple black outfit, a narrow chiffon scarf at her throat. Her clothing and the little jewelry she wore were less expensive and more conservative than the things the rest of the ladies were wearing, and it was obvious even to Andrew that she had paid less attention to her hair and makeup than the rest of the throng. She looked somewhat out of place in the glittering room.

There was a reason for the difference, of course. Dr. Beth Popik, in contrast to the society ladies, worked for a living—she was one of the top researchers at the Nichols BioTech Institute, the beneficiary of the Books and Bachelors Luncheon. It was customary for a couple of the more senior women at the institute to attend the luncheon as guests of the organizing committee.

Finally, she regained her voice. "That's okay," she said, attempting to sound brisk. "Please don't worry about it." Beth Popik was more shaken by the brief encounter than she should have been, as if there had been some kind of spark between her and Andrew.

"My apologies," Andrew managed to say, before Jackie ushered him away again. The woman stared after him as he went, the expression on her face a curious combination of fascination and concern.

Then, from behind her, came a voice she recognized: "Well, I never figured you for the charity auction type, Beth."

Beth Popik turned and came face-to-face with Dr. Kate Calder, a fellow researcher at Nichols BioTech. Standing side by side, Beth appeared insignificant, with her drab brown hair and pale complexion, while Kate overshadowed her with a hard countenance and severe, dark good looks.

Despite the fact that the women were not friends—in fact, they were intense and unrelenting rivals—Beth did manage a smile, cold though it might have been. She was not quite sure why Kate disliked her so much—they were engaged in similar research, and so Calder must have considered Beth to be a threat. But Kate's antagonism toward her did not bother her much. As far as she could tell, Kate Calder didn't like anyone at Nichols BioTech, and nobody who worked there ever expressed any affection for Dr. Calder.

Kate didn't mind being disliked, but one could tell from looking at Beth that she was intimidated by her competitor, fearing her sharp tongue and steely manner. Nevertheless, she managed to answer with a certain amount of aplomb.

"Well, Kate," she said evenly, "everybody has to eat lunch. Besides, I was invited by Jackie Cysse and the organizing committee, as were you, I would imagine."

Kate Calder did not even stop, breezing by her, tossing a comment over her shoulder as she went. "Well," she said, "it's up to you, Beth. You know . . . if you think you can afford the time."

"I didn't see you in the lab today," Beth shot back. "I did a few hours' work this morning."

This time Kate did stop and turn, but she did not look Beth in the eye. Instead her eyes swept the room, as if looking for someone more important in the crowd.

"That's very nice, Beth. Very dedicated of you. I'm sure you're making great strides in your research."

"Well, what are *you* doing here, Kate?" Beth asked.

"I figured that if anybody here had any serious questions about the institute, there ought to be someone here who could answer them." There wasn't even a smile on Kate's face to lessen the impact of the words. They hit Beth like little darts, each one of them stinging as they struck.

Beth opened her mouth to say something in reply, but Kate had swept on, and Jackie was at the podium now, calling the luncheon to order.

"Ladies! Ladies!" she said into the microphone, her voice filling the room. "Please take your seats. Ladies! *Ladies!* And the gentlemen, too, of course!"

Kate Calder found her seat and sat down, but paid little attention to her tablemates or to the proceedings of the luncheon. She was lost in her own thoughts, thinking, as she did almost all the time, about the future. Her snide little remark to Beth Popik—the one about being able to spare the time—may have sounded nasty to her colleague, but it had not been directed at her. Rather, it had been a reminder to herself—a way of telling herself she had no idea how much time she had left.

Chapter Three

*J*ackie was in her element, up there at the podium, running the luncheon like the conductor of a symphony orchestra. She was completely comfortable in her role even though every eye in the room was on her. Andrew, by contrast, was still feeling terribly self-conscious as he took his seat with the other bachelors at the table right down front.

The other men at the table seemed blithely unconcerned about the upcoming auction—Andrew got the distinct feeling that a couple of them were actually looking forward to it—but he could not escape his own feelings of unease.

Despite all the talk of doing this for a good cause, he felt that there was something slightly indecorous about the proceedings he was about to become part of.

"Good news!" Jackie announced from the podium. "Our book sale has just sold out!"

There was a smattering of light applause as Jackie continued. "And we are very pleased to have with us today some of those dedicated doctors whose research will be directly affected by the tax-free donations you have made today."

Jackie scanned the crowd until her eyes lit on a certain table. "Will you stand, please? Dr. Katherine Calder and Dr. Beth Popik."

Kate stood and waved rather halfheartedly. Beth stood and felt the blood rush to her face; she felt plain and awkward and she disliked being the center of attention. At least her moment in the limelight lasted no longer than a second or two.

Jackie quickly moved on to other business—the amount of money raised so far and the calendar of events coming up in the course of the year that would raise even more. Finally, she ended her speech, and lunch was served.

Andrew noticed that there were two selections for the meal: a very small piece of chicken or a very small piece of fish, both grilled. Andrew chose the fish, and while he ate, he listened to the talk around the table.

The other men seated there seemed to know one another, all of them veterans of the society charity circuit and well acquainted with their hostess. Andrew learned that Jackie was the second wife—"trophy wife" they said—of the late Harvey Cysse. The deceased tycoon had divorced his first wife, a woman who had raised their four children and stood by him through thick and thin for forty years, before marrying Jackie. The seventy-five-year-old groom and the thirty-six-year-old bride had enjoyed wedded bliss for just over a year before Harvey died. By then he had rewritten his will to make his widow extremely rich.

"They say she got five units," said a handsome young man who turned out to be an investment banker attached to a very prestigious Wall

Street firm. There were low whistles from the other men seated around the table.

"That's some really serious money," said one of the men. "I wonder who she invests with."

But Andrew had no idea what they were talking about. "Five units?" he asked, looking up from his plate. "Five units of what?"

"You know, a unit," said the young man from Wall Street. "A unit is a hundred million dollars, and she got five of them."

"Half a billion dollars?" said Andrew. Money didn't mean much to angels—they knew how insignificant it really was in the greater scheme of things. "Why would anyone need that much money?"

The rest of the men at the table laughed, assuming he was making an extremely dry joke.

"Yeah," said the Wall Streeter. "*Really . . .*"

Desserts were not popular at charity luncheons. The *tarte tatin* served to Andrew seemed to be the size of a large button. The espresso was served in a cup scarcely larger.

No sooner had the last plate been removed

than the *real* fun of the afternoon began. Conversation died down a bit when Jackie walked back to the podium and tapped the microphone to get the attention of everyone present.

"Well," she said, "let's get started." She gestured toward Andrew's table, crooking a finger at one of the men there. "Come on up here, Hugh."

Hugh stood up, winked quickly, and stage-whispered to the rest of his tablemates, "Wish me luck, guys."

Jackie continued at the podium. "I'd like you to meet Dr. Hugh Brooks, who has kindly agreed to be our first bachelor today! Now, I know this is what you've all been waiting for. So let the bidding begin! Dr. Hugh, come on up here." There was spirited applause as Hugh Brooks made his way up to the auction block. Andrew had never felt such embarrassment and could only sink down in his chair, cover his eyes, and *wish* this weren't happening to him.

Jackie was an old pro at these auctions and she kept the bidding moving along at a good clip, interjecting jokes and observations about the bidders and the men up for auction. She cajoled and wheedled and, in a good-natured sort of way, sweet-talked the richest women in the room into paying top dollar for the privilege of a date with one of the bachelors. When the bidding slowed down, Jackie got it started again; when things got out of hand, she calmed things down a bit, reining in overly high spirits. One by one the bachelors were auctioned off until Andrew was the last man sitting at the table. The men had "sold" for between $3,500 and $5,000 each. Andrew, now sunk so low in his chair he was almost lying on his back, thought he would be lucky if he fetched more than a dollar.

The penultimate bachelor was standing at the auction block, a broad smile on his face. It seemed that this young man was actually *enjoying* his moment in the spotlight. "This is Assistant District Attorney Peter Carpenter, ladies. Who will open the bidding at one thousand dollars?"

No sooner had the words left her mouth than someone at the back of the room shouted, "One thousand . . ."

Bidding climbed quickly, but stalled at three thousand dollars. "That's too low," Jackie announced. "Do I hear thirty-five hundred? Ladies! A night on the town with one of the city's most eligible bachelors? Thirty-five hundred, please . . ."

"Thirty-five hundred!" someone shouted.

"Yes!" said Jackie, punching the air triumphantly. "Thirty-five hundred there in the back. Going once. Going twice . . . sold! Thirty-five hundred dollars for Assistant District Attorney Peter Carpenter. A bargain price for a great guy. Have a wonderful time, you two!"

Peter Carpenter stepped off the stage and walked through the crowd to meet his date. The two embraced and kissed.

Andrew looked up to see Jackie summoning him to the stage. He heaved a great big sigh, then got to his feet slowly.

From a table in the rear of the room, Dr. Beth Popik was watching Andrew intently; Kate Calder, on the other hand, stifled a yawn and checked her watch while she prepared to make a quiet, unobtrusive, early exit. This society nonsense was precisely the sort of thing that bored her to tears. But when office rumors had told her that Beth was going to be there, she had decided to tamp down her reverse snobbism and show up, if only to find out what was going on with her colleague. She was positive that Beth would not be bidding on a bachelor. That was just not the kind of thing that the shy Dr. Popik would dream of doing.

Kate realized that Beth had come for no particularly significant reason and that she was now free to leave. Something of a relief, she thought, ever so slightly grateful to Beth's sense of insecurity and fear of the future. Kate paid no attention to what was going on up there onstage.

This little society circus would bring in a bit of money for the Nichols Institute—that was the important thing. Other than that, there was no reason for Kate to be there a moment longer.

Jackie positioned Andrew at the podium and flashed him her most winning smile. "And now," she said, "I am delighted to introduce our last bachelor, Dr. Andrew Friend. Now, Andy has been a close friend of our family for years . . ."

Andrew started as if he had been pinched. This was definitely news to him. He caught a glimpse of Tess and Monica—both were shaking their heads in disbelief, but were still managing to hold back their laughter.

Jackie put an arm around Andrew's waist and hugged him. "I love him like my own . . . younger brother," she announced. "I wish he *had* been my younger brother."

Everyone, including Jackie herself, laughed out loud, but Andrew turned an even deeper shade of crimson. He could not believe that this was happening to him.

"And I want you to know," Jackie continued, saying the first things that popped into her head, "that Andy here is a dedicated physician who, by the way, dances a pretty mean rumba."

More news to Andrew.

"Ladies," Jackie went on, "believe me when I tell you that after a date with Andy you'll never be the same."

"Well," Tess whispered to Monica, "at least

that part is true." It was difficult to imagine a meeting with The Angel of Death that *didn't* change your life—and rather drastically at that.

Jackie waited for the laughter to die down, then got down to business. She was determined to end the auction with a real bang. She was going to do her best to get a high price for her new pal, Dr. Andrew Friend.

"Do I have an opening bid of two thousand dollars?" Jackie asked as she scanned the room, looking for women she knew had not bid on anyone that day and who could afford to open their pocketbooks wide and pay big.

There was a moment of silence. Then, from the back of the room, the usually introverted Beth Popik heard her own voice say: "Two thousand dollars!" She seemed dazed, not quite able to believe that she had actually said it.

Just as amazed as Beth was Kate. She stared at her competitor for a moment, then looked up at Andrew, checking him out for the first time. It was obvious that she was thinking of getting into a bidding war. But before she could make an offer, yet another voice piped up.

"Twenty-five hundred!" Monica suddenly shouted.

Jackie looked delighted. "Twenty-five! That's great! But it's not enough!" she announced. "Come on now, do I hear three thousand dollars out there?"

Now it was Tess' turn to be shocked. "Just what do you think you're doing, Monica?"

"I don't want him to feel cheap," Monica explained. "You can understand that, can't you?"

"Well . . . ," said Tess reluctantly. "I *guess* I can. Seems like a waste of money, though, if you ask me."

"Just watch what happens," whispered Monica. "I'm guessing Andrew's price will skyrocket now."

Her words seemed to pay off immediately. The bid from Monica spurred Beth on. Her heart was pounding, and she was sure she was doing something completely crazy, but the words came out of her mouth anyway. "Three thousand!"

Kate Calder could not help but notice the urgency in the bid of her rival. Something inside her threw her into the bidding. It was a nasty thing to do—she knew that—but she could not help herself. If Beth wanted this guy, then Kate had to do her best to see that she didn't get him. Childish, foolish—maybe so. But somehow it was also deeply satisfying.

"Thirty-five hundred!" the usually austere, no-nonsense doctor shouted. She even rose a little bit out of her gilded chair as she yelled out her bid. Beth stared at Kate—she couldn't believe that her fellow doctor and researcher had bid on *her* man.

"I have a bid of thirty-five hundred dollars on the rumba master, Dr. Andrew Friend," Jackie announced. "That's nice, ladies. Very nice. But not enough!"

But Jackie knew that was just bravado on her part. She was pretty sure it would go no farther than that and that the bidding for Andrew was pretty much done. After all, she reasoned, no one knew him; he had no special social claims on any of the women there—thirty-five hundred was about the best she figured her last-minute replacement bachelor would do. Not bad, considering the circumstances. True, he was a doctor and, yes, he was good-looking, but he didn't have the prestige of her original choice, the eminent cardiologist, Dr. Ray Hannah. *He,* she was sure, would have topped out at somewhere around five thousand dollars—at the very *least.*

But, for once, Jackie Cysse had made a mistake, reading this particular hand of cards—social cards—incorrectly. No sooner had the thirty-five-hundred-dollar bid come in than it was topped by a bigger bid.

Beth glared across the room at Kate. Why would she bother to bid so high? Beth never thought that she would spend money on anything so frivolous. Kate never acted interested in anything that would keep her from her precious research.

Beth's features hardened as the truth dawned on her. Kate was doing what she was doing only to annoy her, to spoil her own plans. From the moment Beth had seen Andrew, when they bumped into each other, she had felt some connection to him. She felt that she *had* to know him better. She couldn't explain why exactly, but she knew that money wasn't going to hold her back. Without hesitation she raised her voice. "I bid four thousand dollars!"

Kate was dumbfounded at Beth's persistence, but she wasn't going to be stopped either. She snapped back immediately, calling out her own bid. "Four thousand five hundred dollars!"

Kate sat back in her little gold chair and smiled at the people around her, sure that she had announced the winning bid. Her tablemates whispered congratulations and smirked behind their hands. Kate Calder was no one's idea of a fun date. She was blunt to the point of rudeness and completely obsessed by her work. The poor bachelor had no idea what he was in for if Kate proved triumphant.

Kate, of course, had other plans, which did not include going on a date with the guy, should she win. Maybe when this doctor—what was his name anyway?—was brought down to her she would pay the bill and present him to Beth as a gift. Yes . . . that would be the most humiliating thing she could do. She was looking forward to making her grand gesture when Beth piped up again.

Doctors who choose medical research over the private practice of medicine don't have a lot of money to throw away on society auctions. And while it's true that even doctors engaged in research are paid better than most people, research physicians never ascend into the realms of the serious money—the stratospheric incomes of the society dermatologists, the sports medicine specialists, and the plastic surgeons who cater to the whims and complaints of the very rich. So the money that Kate and Beth were throwing around represented significant pieces of their income.

But Beth wanted to buy "Dr. Andrew Friend," and she didn't care how much he cost. The odd thing was she didn't really know why. All she knew was that the look in his blue eyes had told her something—it hadn't been undying love or anything else as obvious or as pedestrian—but she *knew* that there was something about him that touched her, touched her soul. Something she needed to know more about. And if money was the medium that would bring her that answer, she would spend it. And she would spend it gladly.

The price was too rich for Beth, but she announced it anyway, and spoke the price proudly: "Five thousand dollars!"

When Tess heard the figure she half-turned to Monica and whispered in her ear, "So much for your fears . . . thinking he was going to feel cheap."

"Shh," Monica replied quickly. "It's not over yet, you know. He could fetch a lot more."

The rest of the crowd was impressed by the five-thousand-dollar bid. There was a certain amount of oohing and aahing from the spectators, as well as some applause. In the audience a dozen women—women far richer than Kate and Beth—wondered if they should get involved. Plainly this Dr. Andrew Friend was a find—a find who happened to be a friend of Jackie Cysse. Every one of them knew that giving Jackie a hand would pay back in spades in the social sphere.

"Five thousand dollars for the extremely desirable Dr. Andrew Friend," Jackie Cysse announced, her wide blue eyes glittering with delight. "That can't possibly be enough, ladies . . . Do I hear fifty-five hundred dollars for this wonderful prize? And that's cheap!"

Andrew was not used to hearing himself described as a wonderful prize; even those souls who welcomed him when he came for them at the end of their lives did not consider him a prize . . . well, not *exactly*. This auction was even worse than he had dared to imagine. He could feel his cheeks burning with embarrassment, and he just wished the whole thing were over and done.

Kate didn't think she wanted to bid a dime more than she had already. So, for a moment, it looked as if Beth had won the day and the prize, but then something in her rival made her speak up.

Kate Calder struck again—maybe it was her dislike of Beth, maybe it was her unwillingness to be outdone in anything, but something in Kate made her decide to bid again, to up the ante one more time.

Kate shouted her bid: "Six thousand dollars!"

There were gasps around the room. Beth sighed heavily—she could bid no more. She had already gone far past her budget. But Kate smiled in triumph. Jackie looked delighted and glanced over at Beth to see if she had any advance on the six-thousand-dollar bid. But despite Beth's strange attraction to Andrew, she knew that she could not afford to pay any more money than she had already bid. Five thousand was probably too much. Reluctantly she shook her head when Jackie looked at her, and then looked away.

"Six thousand dollars!" Jackie Cysse crowed. She raised her gavel. "Going once. Going twice . . . sold!" She brought the gavel down with a loud crack, and there was immediate and prolonged applause at the high bid of the day.

Beth was genuinely disappointed, but Kate did not seem to notice her triumph or even care about it. She was digging in her purse for her checkbook as Andrew climbed down from the auction block, making his way toward the winning bidder.

Jackie wrapped things up quickly. "Thank

you, everyone!" she said. "That wonderful bid ends this year's Books and Bachelors Luncheon. And I know we'll be seeing you all right back here next year."

As far as Jackie was concerned, that was the end of the event. She had no idea what her little charity luncheon had set in motion.

Chapter Four

Andrew caught up with Kate as she stood at the cashier's desk to the left of the podium. She had her head down and was busily writing out the check to the charity. As she made out the check that paid for her time with her impulse purchase, she did not so much as glance in his direction. She didn't mind spending the money—beating out her arch-rival Beth Popik had held its usual pleasure—but she had no intention of spending the time with her "eligible bachelor." Far from it. Her only intention had been to win one more small victory in the continuing war she had declared on Beth.

Of course, Andrew had no idea of any of this when he caught up with her. He approached warily, as if afraid of startling her, the way a hunter avoids spooking an animal.

"Hi," he said with a half smile. He was feeling awkward and unpolished, completely unsure of himself. It was safe to say that he was not certain what the protocol was for this sort of thing. Besides, he was far from used to going on dates. "I'm Andrew . . ."

Kate glanced at him, a cold, dismissive glance, and went on writing her check. She ripped it from the checkbook and handed it to the cashier.

The cashier took it. "Just a minute, ma'am," the woman said, "I'll give you a receipt."

"Don't bother," said Kate. She turned and, still studiously ignoring Andrew, made for the door. Andrew sighed and followed along in her wake. He steeled himself against her indifference and caught up with her.

"Miss Calder?" said Andrew. "I guess I'm not really sure what happens next. Maybe you could enlighten me. I've never been auctioned off before."

60

Kate paused and stared at him coldly. "You know," she said finally, "I think I know practically every doctor in this town . . . and I've never heard of you, Dr. Andrew Friend. I can't help but wonder why that is. Of course, a friend of Jackie Cysse's is bound to be well known—and I have the feeling you're not." She looked at him critically for a second or two. "Am I right . . . '*Doctor*'?"

"Well," said Andrew, feeling the harshness of her gaze, "that's something I want to explain to you . . . And I thought doing so over dinner would be the perfect opportunity."

Kate Calder stopped and looked him up and down, her face hard and unsmiling. "Look," she said, her words clipped and cold, "nothing personal, but I'm not interested in a date with you. I spent the money because it goes to a good cause, so let's just forget it, okay, *Dr. Friend*?"

Andrew shook his head slightly, like a boxer shaking off a blow. "But I don't understand," he said. "If you didn't want to go out, why didn't you just make a donation to the institute? Why did you bother to bid for me?"

"I wasn't bidding for you," Kate said bluntly. She had never had a problem with being frank.

"You weren't?" Andrew asked. Somewhere inside him he felt a sense of hurt. It surprised him. He thought that the auction was the most humiliating thing he had ever undergone, but having emerged from it triumphant with the top bid, he was now determined to see it through. He knew this must be part of the assignment—there was no way he could have been placed in this position without good reason. And he was sure that his desire to dine with this infuriating woman was certainly not based on vanity on his part.

"No, I wasn't bidding for you," Kate explained. "I was bidding against her." She cocked her head toward Beth Popik, who was walking up the stairs and out of the room. At that moment, Beth stopped and turned, as if she knew she was being talked about. As she glanced back at them, her eyes alighting on Andrew, she felt once again that peculiar feeling, that stab of recognition, the sense that somehow, from somewhere, she knew him.

Kate was oblivious to Beth's gaze. "And I won," she said. She looked pleased at her success, but Andrew could not help but see the sadness in her eyes. Kate walked away, leaving Andrew in a state of total confusion.

The angels were assembled in a corner of the hotel lobby, going over the rather puzzling—but to Tess and Monica, very entertaining—events of the afternoon.

"I don't get it," said Andrew, with a shake of his head. "This makes no sense at all. Why would she spend all that money just to annoy someone she works with?"

"That seems extremely mean-spirited of her," said Monica. "And on top of that" she added, "it seems like you went through that whole thing for nothing."

Andrew was surprised to discover that he was feeling a little defensive about that.

"Well, I *did* get the highest price of any guy

there, you know," he said in his own defense. "And as you keep saying, it was in aid of a good cause. That counts for something, surely."

It was obvious that Tess was not interested in debating the smaller points of the Books and Bachelors Luncheon; she was more interested in the big picture. "I've got a feeling it was more than that, Andrew . . . I've got the feeling it was for more than we know." She looked to Monica and Andrew, the seriousness showing in her eyes. "There's a reason we were all called here. I'm sure of it."

This gave Monica and Andrew pause. They had long ago learned to trust Tess' intuition in these matters. The sheer weight of Tess' centuries of experience gave great import to any feelings she might have. There was silence for a moment before Monica noticed a familiar figure striding across the hotel lobby, coming toward them.

"Adam?" said Monica. She glanced over at Tess. "What's Adam doing here?" she asked, more puzzled than ever. "I didn't know he was assigned to work with us."

Tess shook her head slowly. "Neither did I."

Like Andrew, Adam was an Angel of Death. He was a little older-looking, perhaps a little more urbane and sophisticated. He was dressed as formally as Andrew, but he seemed more at ease in his finery than Andrew was in his. For an Angel of Death he was something of a charmer.

"I am so sorry," said Adam, coming up to where the angels were sitting. "Monica, you're looking lovely! Am I too late?"

"Well," said Tess sternly, "that depends." She did not approve of tardiness in the angels under her supervision. "What are you talking about?"

"I had a passing in Duluth," Adam said a touch defensively. Tess could be hard on her angels. "A charming, delightful lady, all her affairs in order," Adam said. "Ninety-two years old, and she couldn't wait to go home." He smiled beatifically. "And I was all ready to take her and then, poof, *Wheel of Fortune* comes on . . ."

"*Wheel of Fortune?*" Tess said with a snort.

"What on earth does *Wheel of Fortune* have to do with anything?"

Adam smiled. "What on *earth*, Tess? Well, it turned out the last thing she wanted to see on earth was the bonus round in *Wheel of Fortune*. She wouldn't go until it was over."

Andrew nodded as the picture became clear. "Oh, I get it. You were delayed, so I was sent here to cover for you."

Adam nodded. "That's right. Thanks."

"But we still don't know what the assignment is," said Monica. "Or why Tess and I are here."

"Wait, wait," said Adam, holding up a hand, like a policeman stopping traffic. "Not so fast . . ." He turned back to Andrew. "Andrew, did you stand here and get randomly chosen to be a bachelor?"

Andrew nodded. "Yes. That's right. I didn't like it."

"You're not supposed to like it, Andrew," said Adam with a smile. "It's all part of the plan . . . And then did the doctor bid on you?"

"Yeah," said Andrew ruefully. "I fetched six

66

thousand bucks. The highest bid, as it turned out."

Adam laughed. "Not bad, not bad at all. I'm not saying I wouldn't have fetched a bit more, but six thousand dollars—that's pretty impressive."

"Get on with it," growled Tess.

"Okay," said Adam. "So, the date's on? It's all set up for tonight, then?"

Andrew shook his head. "If that's the plan, then it didn't work. She blew me off."

Suddenly Adam was more than a little alarmed. "No," he said urgently. "You have to go on that date with her tonight."

"I don't think she likes me," said Andrew with a little smile. "Maybe you ought to go instead."

Adam shook his head. "No, that won't work. You're the angel on the case now. You've got to follow through on this." He reached inside his jacket pocket and pulled out a small business card. "Here's the restaurant you're supposed to take her to." He glanced down at Tess and Monica. "And I think you're going to need some backup on this one, Andrew."

"We still don't know what we're supposed to do, Adam," said Monica. "We've had no instructions at all."

Adam cleared his throat nervously. "Well, I think you'll know what to do when you see the restaurant." He snuck a quick peek at his wristwatch. "Look, I've got a scuba diving crisis in three minutes. I may be a while—it could go either way. I'll meet you at the restaurant tonight and fill you in." He looked sternly at Andrew and wagged his finger at him. "Just make sure you get her there."

Then Adam turned on his heel and made for the double glass doors of the hotel lobby—but never emerged on the other side. He had vanished. The three angels exchanged a look.

"What do you make of that?" Monica asked.

"I don't know," said Andrew, standing up and straightening his suit coat. "But I have to get out of here."

"Where are you going?" Tess asked.

"Hey," said Andrew, "I guess I need a date for tonight."

Chapter Five

*I*t had been an expensive day for Dr. Kate Calder.

First she had the unexpected expenditure at the Books and Bachelors Luncheon, now she was paying for the installation of an extremely high-tech safe in her corner of the lab at the Nichols BioTech research laboratory. There was no shortage of safes and locked, fireproof file cases at Nichols, but Kate had insisted on having her own strongbox, and she was determined to pay for it out of her own pocket. In paying for her own security, Kate bought the right to have sole knowledge of the combination. The expensive, electronic safe—it was absolutely top of the line—was known around the institute as "Kate's Folly," and already engendered a certain amount of resentment; it suggested that Kate did not trust her colleagues with her precious research. But that was par for the course with the difficult Dr. Calder.

Kate made no secret of her dislike for her associates, and it was only the quality of her work that allowed her to be tolerated by the management of the institute and those around her.

Science labs are frequently studies in contrasts. There is almost always intense personal competition between individuals or even between teams of researchers working on the same project. But the opposite can also be true. Inside the lab there might be competition, but there is also a sense of belonging, a sense that, in the end, it is all about teamwork. They are, after all, a band of professionals engaging in serious work—work that might have a significant impact on the greater world.

But Kate was not a part of that team. Competition was the driving force behind her work, which left no room for friends. She *never* had any friends. Orphaned at two, she had no recollection of her parents. She had never felt a part of anything. She was sent to live with an elderly aunt, her sole living relation, who followed her parents to the grave several years later.

Her first experience with foster parents was a disappointment. After the recent loss of all of her blood relatives, Kate searched for a place to belong and for someone to love her. Still struggling with her grief, she firmly believed that her foster parents could provide the home she longed for. However, the adoption of a beautiful six-month-old baby girl replaced her standing in her new "family" and she was passed along to another foster home. By that time Kate was a sullen, hardened eight-year-old who did nothing to endear herself to would-be adoptive parents.

By her early teens she was a ward of the state and was sent to live in an orphanage, living in a dormitory with thirty-two other morose, tough girls. But instead of going down the path of most of the other girls—rebellion, drugs, fights, early pregnancy, repeated attempts to escape—

71

Kate worked out her own, more subtle code of defiance. She had been determined to escape that dispiriting place, but she wasn't going to do it by crudely knotting together her bedsheets and making a break for the nearest boy, bar, or bus station.

Young Kate had a plan. And she was smart enough to see that her plan would work. The young, friendless girl took a good, hard look at her world and discovered that it was the *winners* who got what they wanted in life. Rebelliousness, blindly striking out at authority, might feel good for a moment, it might even make other sulky, disaffected girls look up to you and think you're cool. But Kate knew that to really get away, to *really* escape the system, you had to play the system against itself.

She knew she had to play it cool and obey all the rules to the letter, no matter how petty or silly she might consider them. She had to risk the goody-two-shoes image and the taunts and ostracism that went along with it.

Kate threw herself into schoolwork, racing through grades at ridiculous speed. She skipped grades twice, once in junior high and once in high school. By the time she was a senior she was auditing classes at a local college.

A girl of no background, money, or even parents, Kate was courted by colleges all over the country, all of them offering full scholarships. She chose MIT, went to Johns Hopkins Medical School, and did her residency at Peter Bent Brigham in Boston. Once she was a newly minted doctor, she turned her back on lucrative private practice and went into pure research. This brought her to Nichols BioTech, her research, and her absurdly complicated safe.

If anyone had bothered to think about the makeup of Kate's cranky disposition, they would have been forced to surmise that she was this way because she had been alone much of her life and had fought tooth-and-nail for everything she had. But they would have overlooked one simple thing about this tough young woman: she had never known a moment of love. No one had ever loved her, and she had never loved anyone else. There was an empty space inside of her where those feelings should have been . . .

She was wearing a white lab coat over the suit she had worn to the luncheon and was watching the man installing the safe put the final touches on the LED display lock. The safe was certainly an impressive-looking one and yet another way Kate telegraphed to her fellow workers: I'm better than you are.

"Okay," the installer said, standing up. "You're all set. Just type in your password—I won't look—and that'll lock this baby up tighter than Fort Knox."

Kate looked around the room, making sure that no one was watching her. Beth was working at the far end of the lab, but seemed to be ignoring the little ceremony. Kate punched the code into the keypad. The sequence of numbers were the only ones from her past that meant anything—the date of the death of her parents. This was as close as she would ever get to raising a memorial to them. That done, she stood up and regarded the strongbox as if it were something sacred, like an altar or a reliquary.

As if she knew that it was now safe to take in what was going on there on the far side of the room, Beth looked up from her work and gazed over at Kate and her new, state-of-the-art safe. It was plain that Beth was offended that Kate trusted no one at Nichols and thought her colleagues would stoop to stealing data.

And besides, weren't they all working toward a common goal? Weren't they supposed to be *teammates*? Beth walked over and looked at the safe, then at Kate, who clutched some files to her chest, as if she were afraid Beth would snatch them from her.

"That's pretty heavy security, isn't it?" asked Beth. "I think it's a shame that you think you need it."

"Well, at least I have something to protect," Kate replied, a little smirk playing on her lips.

Beth shook her head and walked away. Her story wasn't quite as dramatic as Kate's, but there were similarities. She lived alone—except for her big dog, Bruno—in a little house in Westchester, a county just north of the city. She had few friends; she had been bookish as a child and had excelled in college when her classmates chose to do just okay and have some fun. Beth didn't have a lot of fun, but she didn't have the anger that Kate possessed.

As she left she heard Kate asking the installer a question that showed the depths of her paranoia.

"What if somebody tries to break in?" she asked. "Could that be done?"

He shook his head and laughed at the question. "Houdini himself couldn't break into this baby, lady. If somebody starts guessing the code and punches in the wrong numbers, the whole system will freeze up for a full twelve hours. Even you won't be able to get in until the time is up."

Kate put her files into the safe, then punched her multidigit code into the keypad. Instantaneously, the readout came up on the LED screen: "System Locked."

The safe installer looked around the lab and sort of mock-shivered in fright. "This is the first time I've ever done an installation in a place like this," he said. "Mostly I do offices and jewelers."

"Really," said Kate, indicating that she did not have the slightest interest in the man's conversational gambit, and even less interest in his profession.

The poor fellow didn't know that, of course, so he sailed on. "So, whaddya got in there?" the workman continued, with a smile on his face. "One of those scary viruses that kill people in about two minutes flat?"

Kate did not have much of a sense of humor even at the best of times and, as one might expect, she *never* joked about her work. She did not respond directly to the weak little joke the workman made.

"Thank you for your help," she said with a sour look on her face—a look that did not escape the workman. Now he knew all he needed to know about Dr. Calder. He shrugged, picked up his toolbox, and headed for the door. As he left the room he passed Andrew coming in. It took a moment for Kate to look up and notice him, but, when she did, she was not at all pleased to see him.

"Oh, *really*. This is too much," Kate said wearily. "What on earth are you doing here? I really did not expect to see you again. You are persistent—I'll give you that."

The sudden appearance of the man Beth knew as Dr. Andrew Friend in the Nichols BioTech lab gave rise to a strange feeling again. It wasn't as strong as love or longing—it was more like a sudden and bright happiness one feels when one unexpectedly runs into an old friend.

Kate noticed Beth's interest in her visitor. She was aware that her fellow researcher could not take her eyes off Andrew, and that gave Kate a small frisson of pleasure. But beyond that she did not need to have this guy around, mooning over her and, worst of all, keeping her from her work.

"I know you said to forget about dinner," he said, "but it just doesn't seem fair. I mean, think about what you're missing."

Kate gave him a quick once-over look and Andrew knew that she wasn't crazy about what she was seeing. She shook her head and rolled her eyes.

"You have got to be kidding," she said acidly. "That's a joke, right?" Kate might not have a great sense of humor, but she could at least *identify* a joke when she heard one.

"Well, I didn't mean me," said Andrew quickly.

Modesty came naturally to him. "I mean . . . not necessarily."

"You didn't?" Kate snapped back. "Surely you aren't thinking of bringing another eligible bachelor along?"

"No," he said. "Nothing like that." Andrew smiled.

"What then?" Kate countered. "Explain to me what I might be missing."

Andrew took a deep breath. "What I mean, Dr. Calder, is really quite simple."

Kate couldn't help but be intrigued. "How so?"

"Well," said Andrew, "wouldn't you like to have the satisfaction of coming into work tomorrow after a six-thousand-dollar date and letting everybody go crazy wondering if it was worth it?" He glanced around the room at the others working there and lowered his voice. He found that he enjoyed teasing her.

"And . . . it will be," Andrew said. "But you don't have to tell them that. You'd just keep 'em guessing. Which, I suspect, is something you like to do a lot."

"You suspect?" Kate countered. "What do you mean?"

"Well, take that safe, for example. It's a really impressive one, by the way." His eyes swept the room. "You know, I've seen a lot of vaults, and that is by far the most sophisticated one I've ever seen. You must be the envy of your coworkers. They don't seem to have safes as nice as that one."

Kate half smiled—she knew that Andrew was needling her, and she was surprised at herself. Surprised to find that she actually liked it, or rather, *almost* liked it. She snuck a quick peek at the other scientists in the lab, all of whom were working away at their lab tables and giving the impression of purposefully *not* looking at Kate and her six-thousand-dollar date.

Kate found that Andrew's words were already coming true. She discovered, to her surprise, that she was enjoying the curiosity that seemed to absolutely *radiate* from her diligently nonchalant coworkers. How much more intense would their interest be after her big night out with the date she had purchased? Kate sort of liked it already.

"Come on," Andrew urged her. "It'll be lots of fun. And if you don't mind my saying so, you look like the kind of person who has a definite deficiency in the fun department."

It wasn't the first time Kate had been told that she was no fun, and she didn't mind. What she did mind was being deceived. And she was pretty sure that Andrew was trying to trick her into a date. Men, Kate thought, just had no clue. And the male ego was unassailably stupid—something that had to be drilled through with industrial-strength tools. Kate had learned these lessons long ago.

"Is that it?" Kate countered hotly. "Or is it your insufferable male ego? You just can't imagine, just can't *believe,* that there's a woman on earth who wouldn't want to go out with you."

"I can assure you," said Andrew in mock solemnity, "that male vanity has absolutely nothing to do with my wanting to take you out on the date you paid so dearly for."

Kate thought that he was lying. But, of course, he was telling the absolute truth.

"Yeah, right," said Kate. "You further think that because of the price I paid I secretly want something from you—that I would be a pushover."

Andrew's face turned an embarrassed shade of pink. "I assure you that is not the case either," he said earnestly.

This time, Kate believed him, though she would not have been able to say why. There and then, she decided that she would go out with Andrew—she would not have been able to explain that either. Something in this young man had melted at least the first layer of permafrost in Kate. But she was still Kate Calder and he would have to go a long way and work very hard to get her completely thawed out. Still, the thaw that had progressed this far would have astonished Beth and the rest of Kate's coworkers.

What Andrew did not know was that if Kate was going to go out with him there were going to be some hard-and-fast conditions. Of course, it was perfectly in keeping with that no-nonsense character of hers that the date would take place on terms that she would lay down, or it would not happen at all.

"Okay," she said firmly. "Here are my terms."

Andrew raised an eyebrow. "Terms?"

Kate nodded. "That's right. Terms."

"Fire away."

"It's got to be a nice place," she said firmly. "Expensive and exclusive." Kate rarely went out, and when she did she wanted to make it count. Furthermore, she had already laid out six thousand dollars for this date, and it was in her nature to get value for her money.

Andrew nodded. "It will be very nice," he said, knowing that Tess would be handling the details.

"And this is very important," Kate said resolutely. "I get there myself. I go home alone. Don't get any ideas that because I paid for this, you are entitled to anything else."

"Of course not," said Andrew with a nod. "You're perfectly safe with me. I can assure you of that."

"As long as that is understood," said Kate. "So, where are we going? Chanterelle? Lespinasse?

Gramercy Tavern? Some place like that? I assume you made reservations before the auction, because if you try to get something tonight you are out of luck."

The names of the restaurants meant nothing to Andrew and he did not know how hard it was to get a table in one of the famous places. Getting a dinner reservation at one of New York City's top restaurants was not something that could be procured at the last minute—not unless you had a lot of pull or a very famous name. Not that it was a problem.

"I had someplace else in mind. The address is 508 Madison. Top floor. And don't worry about it—I made reservations."

"Five hundred eight Madison," Kate repeated, her brow furrowed. "That's a new one to me."

"You'll like it," Andrew said. "Trust me."

"Seven o'clock?"

"Great," Andrew said, turning to leave. "See you there."

"Wait!" Kate almost shouted. Andrew stopped. "Is it true—do you really rumba?"

"I will by seven," Andrew said with a wink.

In spite of herself, Kate smiled. She couldn't help it.

Beth watched Andrew go. But she was not smiling. As he went she felt a strange twinge, a sharp jab of sorrow and loss.

Chapter Six

 $\mathcal{F}$ ive hundred eight Madison Avenue was a perfectly ordinary-looking office building at the corner of Fifty-fifth Street. It was, perhaps, the least interesting stretch of Madison Avenue in midtown Manhattan; it came after the Palace Hotel and Saint Patrick's Cathedral, but well before the most chic part of the avenue, the blocks in the sixties and seventies—the part of Madison Avenue that rivaled the Faubourg Saint Honore in Paris and the Via della Spiga in Milan as a fashion center. Up there on Madison where the ladies who lunch shopped for clothes that they wore to the chic restaurants that were,

oddly enough, in exactly the same neighbor-
hood.

The building at 508 Madison Avenue was *not*
the kind of place where one would expect to find
a fine, four-star restaurant in New York City. While
it was true that some New York City skyscrapers
did boast superb restaurants on their top floors,
those buildings tended to be glamorous or famous,
and the restaurants just as well known: Windows
on the World atop the World Trade Center, or
the Rainbow Room, a fixture on the top floor of
Rockefeller Center since the 1930s. Five hundred
eight Madison Avenue simply did not compare.

When Andrew got to the top floor, there
wasn't even a restaurant. Just a torn-up, open
space. It was a mess, a completely unfinished dis-
aster with construction debris scattered in piles
everywhere.

In the middle of all this chaos stood Monica
and Tess. They did not look happy, either, but
they did not look as if they were about to give
in to madness or hysteria. Andrew, on the other
hand, took but one glance around the place and
was absolutely panic-stricken. His jaw dropped,

and he gasped. This dump most emphatically did *not* fit the description of the "nice place" he had promised Kate.

"What is this?" he demanded. "What kind of joke are you trying to play on me?"

"No joke, Andrew," said Monica brightly. "This is going to be your restaurant." She spoke with such conviction that it seemed as if she believed that the restaurant was already there.

Tess was more down-to-earth about the situation. "This is not a restaurant, is what this is," she said dryly. She didn't seem upset at all by the state of the "restaurant." She was just stating the facts.

"But she's coming," said Andrew. "She's going to be here in three hours!"

"Well," said Monica, "we have a problem."

"A problem!" Andrew yelped. "I'd say we have a little more than a problem. We don't even have any chairs!"

"First things first," Monica replied. She seemed extremely calm about the whole thing. "Tess wants to go Italian, but there are so many Italian restaurants in New York, so I was thinking more along the lines of Pacific Rim—what do you think, Andrew?"

Andrew sighed heavily and sank down onto a big, wooden cable spool. "I think it's going to be a very long night." He hated to think what Kate would say when she showed up and got a look at this place. Doubtless, her tongue would be extra sharp.

"Don't worry about it, Angel Boy," said Tess. "Don't worry about a thing."

But Andrew was worried about it. He jumped to his feet and paced the bare room. "This is not happening," he said. "This cannot be happening."

"What are you so nervous about?" Tess asked him. Of course she knew the answer, but she got a little kick out of teasing Andrew. "There's nothing to worry about."

"This is his first date," said Monica with a little smirk. "Everyone is nervous before their first date."

"First date." said Andrew.

"This is *not* a date," Tess growled. "It is an assignment, and I hope you two aren't going to forget it."

Andrew stopped pacing for a moment. "Yeah," he said. "But I've been *assigned* to go on a date. This is serious. Look at this place! I can't bring her in here."

"But this is where you were told to bring her," Monica chimed in. Monica, like Tess, believed that the rules were the rules. If the assignment was to take place in this location, then there was a good reason for it, and they were not to question it.

"I believe it's something called a controlled environment," Monica went on. "Your doctor lady should appreciate that. Scientists like that sort of thing."

Andrew was in no mood to have his leg pulled, not with the catastrophe that was looming before him. "She's in a 'controlled environment' all day," he responded sharply. "And I promised her I would take her someplace really nice. And no matter what you say about this place, 'really nice' is never going to come to mind. At least not to my mind."

Tess' backbone straightened, and she drew herself up to her considerable height. She looked down at Andrew, her eyes blazing with that "Oh ye of little faith" look that Andrew and more than a few other angels had found particularly intimidating over the centuries.

Andrew got a load of Tess' look and felt a little tremor of fear. Somewhere inside his head, he heard a little voice say "Uh-oh."

"Listen up," Tess announced sternly. "God doesn't do cheap, baby. And if I recall, we have been assigned as your backup. So if you will relax and *hush up*, you will be *backed up*. Have you got the picture now, Angel Boy?"

But Andrew didn't get the picture—not right away, at least. "Wait a minute . . . *You* guys are gonna make this happen? You're going to turn this mess into a restaurant by seven o'clock?"

"Yes." Tess crossed her arms across her chest and stared at Andrew balefully. "You got a problem with that?"

Monica stepped up. "The menu is pretty much worked out. We were thinking about a little tower of *salade nicoise* with ahi tuna as an appetizer, then perhaps roasted pheasant over risotto with a lemon sage reduction and just a touch of Asiago cheese, and, let's see, . . . for dessert, a strawberry tart with pistachio filling, topped with vanilla bean sauce and a mocha latte to finish it all off. That would be decaf, of course."

Andrew opened his mouth to say something, thought better of it, then closed it again.

"Any questions?" Tess asked.

Andrew nodded. This time he felt as if he could ask a question without getting his head bitten off. "I have just one question. What is this all for? Do either of you have *any* idea?"

Tess shook her head slowly. "Baby, I don't know. Some lady in Duluth lives a few extra minutes longer so she can watch TV, and she makes an Angel of Death late for an appointment. All of a sudden, I'm cooking dinner in New York and you've got a date with a lady doctor and Monica starts using words like *Asiago*. Now, something has clearly been messed up here, but you know and I know that God is able to straighten it out, which is exactly what I'm sure He's gonna do in His own good time. In the meanwhile—" Tess pointed to something behind him, "Work! For the night is coming!"

Andrew turned to see a broom leaning against the wall. He took a deep breath, took off his jacket, rolled up his sleeves, and did what he was told.

In due course the night did come, and miraculously—in the literal sense of the word—the junk and rubble cluttering the top floor of 508 Madison Avenue were swept away.

A restaurant—and a luxurious one at that—appeared in its place. Tess and her angels had outdone themselves.

There were a main dining room, a bar, and a dance floor, as well as a state-of-the-art, fully equipped professional kitchen. The linens were creamy white and accented with small gold damask flowers; the china was delicately painted with wildflowers, the crystal seemed so delicate it might have been spun from sunlight, and old-fashioned cutlery was silver and heavy.

Chez Tess was the name that Monica had insisted on naming the restaurant, given that Tess would be doing the cooking, and any restaurant lived and died by the skill of the cook. And there was no doubt in Monica's mind that Tess would produce meals that would be nothing short of delectable. It was a complicated way of carrying out an assignment, but the angels did not question it for a moment, as they had complete trust in their Boss. All of the energies of Monica and Tess were geared toward one end: all that had to be done was to produce one delicious meal for two diners, and then Chez Tess could safely go out of business forever.

Tess was ensconced in the kitchen and Monica presided over the "front of the house," stationing herself at the maître d's desk just inside the front door. She was dressed in a dramatic black sheath of silk that ran in a straight line from her shoulder to her ankle, and she wore her hair up for a change. She had never looked lovelier.

Monica was delighted as she looked around at all the details of the beautiful restaurant. The room, filled with fine, old furniture and decorated with heavy, framed pictures seemed more like a rather grand but tastefully decorated private home than a mere restaurant.

Monica felt a little sad that this lovely place would exist for one night only. Wouldn't it be nice, she thought, if they could just *give* the restaurant to some deserving chef when the night was done? But she knew that could not happen.

The view out of the arched windows was nothing short of spectacular. It seemed that every light in every Manhattan skyscraper was burning that night and the sky was lit with a big, yellow, full moon. The soft tinkling of piano music came from the baby grand in the corner, the keys moving by themselves as if played by unseen but skillful hands.

Andrew paced the restaurant nervously, glancing at the antique clock every few seconds, as the old brass hands edged toward the hour of seven o'clock. As the clock began to chime, Kate Calder walked into Chez Tess. It had never occurred to Andrew that his "date" would be nothing if not on time.

Kate was impressed with Chez Tess too. As she walked through the front door of the restaurant, her normally hard features softened for a moment as she took in the gorgeous room. There was a look of wonder in her eyes and she thought that she must have walked into the most romantic restaurant in all of New York City. Of course, if Kate had seen the same place just a few hours before, she would have been even more amazed.

The doctor herself had undergone quite a transformation. Gone was the severely cut suit that she had worn that day. In its place was a red velvet evening gown, accented with a few pieces of expensive jewelry. Gone, too, was the stiff hairstyle that had been pulled back in a tight, professorial bun. Instead she had it down, her dark brown hair falling to her bare shoulders.

Monica could see the look of surprise register on Kate's face, and she felt joy swell inside of her and it almost came pouring out. It was all she could do to maintain the discreet, excessively polite demeanor of a professional headwaiter.

"Good evening," said Monica. "Are you Dr. Calder?" she asked, preserving the fiction. Monica could not imagine anyone else walking through the doors of Chez Tess that evening.

Kate nodded. "Yes, I am Dr. Calder."

"Your table is waiting. This way, please." Monica led the young woman farther into the restaurant. The best table in the place was in the far corner, close to the windows and just to the left of the marble fireplace in which a fire crackled.

Andrew was already waiting there, dressed in a black tuxedo, fiddling with his bow tie and readjusting his cummerbund—an article of clothing he had never worn before. Next to his chair was a bottle of champagne that was sitting in an antique silver ice bucket.

He wished he had more details on this assignment; he felt as if he were flying blind and, for a moment, he considered darting into the kitchen for some last-minute advice from Tess. But then he realized it was too late for that. Monica and Kate were making their way across the room toward him. He stood and pulled out Kate's chair.

"Hi," said Andrew.

"Hi." They shook hands—an awkward, uncertain moment—then Kate slipped into her seat, Andrew into his. Kate looked around the room. For all her attempts to be strictly businesslike, the room and the atmosphere were having the desired effect. She could feel herself relaxing, the cold core inside her melting a bit.

"Shall I open the champagne, sir?" Monica asked. She reached for the bottle chilling in the ice bucket.

"No, thanks," Andrew replied with a smile. "I'll see to it myself, if you don't mind."

"Not at all, sir," said Monica, withdrawing to her post at the door, just like a real maître d'.

Andrew pulled the champagne from the ice bucket and started working on the foil around the neck.

"This is a strange place," said Kate, looking around again. "I've never heard of it."

Restaurants were a minor religion in Manhattan, restaurant reviewers were celebrities, and restaurant reviews were pored over as if they were revealing some universal truths. Diners who wanted to eat in one of the hot new restaurants had to book a month, sometimes two months, in advance. Friends in celebrated kitchens were actively cultivated, because it was an open secret that one celebrity chef could usually free up a table if approached by another celebrity chef.

"It's a pretty new place," said Andrew. "Just opened, really. I sort of stumbled onto it myself."

If only she knew *how* new . . . He held up the bottle of champagne for her inspection.

"Is this okay?" he asked. "Or would you like something else?" He had chosen champagne because he knew it was the kind of drink one took in a place like this. Until that moment, it had never occurred to him that Kate might want something else.

The champagne was a bottle of 1989 Perrier Jouet "Fleur de Champagne," the bottle distinguished by the intricate design of art nouveau flowers painted onto the green glass. Andrew may not have known much about wines, but he had hit the jackpot with this one—there were few champagnes in this class and even fewer that were considered better. And there was an added, more personal bonus in his choice.

Kate beamed when she saw it. "No, nothing else. As a matter of fact, that's my favorite. I have a bottle of it sitting in my refrigerator. It's been there a while now . . . But one day I'll open it. Right now, it's nice to know it's there, because I know that one day I'm going to need it. At least, that's what I hope . . ." She thought a moment. "No. Not hope. I *know* I'm going to need it."

"No kidding?" said Andrew. "Are you going to tell me what you're saving it for? Is there some special occasion coming up? A birthday? An anniversary?"

Kate did not answer, slipping under the question—she knew what the champagne was for, but she didn't want to tell. Not yet, anyway. Andrew noticed her hesitation and knew that there was something very significant in Kate's future, something she was waiting for. He decided not to press her on it.

She countered his question with one of her own. "So, are you a doctor or not? It doesn't matter to me, but I don't think you should go around passing yourself off as one. It's a crime in this state, you know."

101

Andrew did not hesitate. "I'm not a doctor," he said. "And in my own defense, I never claimed that I was. Never passed myself off as one. Jackie Cysse made an assumption that I attempted to correct, but without success. In fact, she sort of rolled right over me like a freight train. She was unstoppable."

Kate smiled. "That is her reputation," she said. "But the charities she works for certainly benefit from her persistence. Nobody can get out the old money and the nouveau riche like Jackie Cysse. If she weren't already so wealthy she could probably make a fortune as a professional fund-raiser or party planner. She certainly has the knack for it."

Andrew knew all about Jackie's fortune. He tore the foil from around the cork of the champagne, then turned his attention to the intricate little wire cage that held the cork in place. There was a small, flat curl of wire tight against the neck. This seemed to be the key to removing the cage.

"So you're not a doctor," said Kate. "That means you didn't treat Jackie's husband, Harvey."

"No," said Andrew. "Although I do know him." He stopped and corrected himself. "I *did* know him. Before he died, that is."

"Well, you would hardly have known him after he died."

"How true."

"So," Kate asked. "Now that we've established that you're not a doctor, do you mind if I ask what it is you really do?"

Andrew paused a moment before answering. This was always a tough question. He was going to have to sit down one day and think up the definitive answer, one that would satisfy everybody and tell the truth at the same time.

"Well," he said after a moment or two, "I guess you could say I'm a sort of counselor. I help people die."

"Ah, I understand," said Kate. She had heard about this modern approach to death and dying. It relied heavily on counselors and grief therapy and working with the person before death to accept death when it was inevitable.

Kate didn't exactly have contempt for the movement—she just didn't have time for it. "I understand. When science fails them, you come in and clean up, is that it? Something like that?" *Dying is dying*, Kate thought. *There is no other way of looking at it.*

"Well, that's one way of putting it," said Andrew, trying to keep the conversation light. But Kate's words were getting darker and the look on her face a little hard. "I give them hope. At least, I try to give them hope."

The word annoyed Kate. "And what do you tell these people about hope? What kind of hope can you give to someone who is so sick they haven't a prayer of recovering?" she asked, bearing down on him as if interrogating him. "I can't help but think that what you do could be considered a little cruel."

Kate thought she had asked a difficult question, but for Andrew there was no easier question to answer.

"Oh," he said, "it's not cruel at all. I tell them that there *is* hope." He shrugged as if the rest of the answer were obvious. "I tell them about God."

"God?" Kate said, as though encountering

the word for the first time. "You tell them about *God*?" She made the notion sound quaint and old-fashioned, as if she, as a doctor, had prescribed leeches or bloodletting to a desperately ill patient.

The wire wrap came off the cork, and Andrew began easing it out of the bottle. "Remember," he said, "I help people die. I don't give them hope about *this* life, Kate. I give them hope about the next life . . . You'd be surprised how interested they are."

His words put Kate on the defensive, and she started to stiffen.

"Ah," she said. "There's something you need to know before we go on with this . . . I don't believe in God." She squared her shoulders. "I believe in science." She spoke proudly, almost boastfully, as if her beliefs were something unique and single to her, as if this were a position that she alone had taken.

But Kate was far from being unique. Andrew had heard these words before. But he knew that truth resonates in a person's spirit and that God's Word never returns void. So he was not discouraged by Kate's cold, hard pronouncement.

"You can't believe in both?" Andrew asked. "Surely there is room for both God and science in a person's life. Not every scientist is an atheist, after all."

"I can only believe in things I can see," Kate replied. "In things I can prove."

"I see . . ." he said, his eyes twinkling. "Well, do you believe in dinner?" He pulled the cork from the neck of the champagne bottle—there was the faintest little pop and then a gentle puff of condensation that looked like blue smoke.

In spite of herself, Kate smiled. "Dinner? Yes, I believe in dinner."

"So do I," Andrew answered. "So I think we should make the first toast to common ground." He poured the champagne into the flutes and handed one to her. "So, here's to a small piece of common ground. A piece of common ground we can both stand on."

Kate nodded. "I can drink to that."

"Good," said Andrew. "It's not much, but it's a start, I suppose. Right?"

"Right," said Kate.

They touched their glasses together lightly in a toast, then they both sipped.

Kate felt the bubbles explode on her tongue. "Hmm," she said appreciatively. "Very, very good champagne." She owned a bottle of it, but she had never actually tasted it. Perrier Jouet "Fleur de Champagne" cost ninety dollars a bottle—a little too much to spend just for a taste of what was to come.

"I'm glad you approve."

Monica had been observing them from her post. They had had their icebreaking chat; the champagne was open. Maybe it was time for them to order. She picked up two menus, the only menus in the restaurant, and walked to the table.

"Welcome to Chez Tess," she said, handing a menu first to Kate, then to Andrew. The menus were carefully written out in exquisite calligraphy with principal letters that looked as if they had been copied from a medieval illuminated manuscript.

"We have a fixed menu, and this is what our chef will be serving this evening . . . ," Monica explained as Kate studied the menu closely. Then, without thinking, Monica continued. "However, if you would like to request a substitution, please don't hesitate to let me know."

Even as she spoke the words, Monica wondered why she was saying them. As far as she knew, Tess was set up in the kitchen for one menu and one menu only. It just *seemed* like the right thing to say, something that a fine New York restaurant would do.

And, as it turned out, Kate did happen to have a number of substitutions in mind. It came as no surprise to Andrew that she would want to make changes in the menu. She had long ago learned that if she wanted something she would have to speak up. No one else would do it for her.

"I would like veal instead of pheasant," she said, handing her menu back to Monica. "And no sage in the lemon reduction, and tea instead of coffee."

Monica did her best to paste a smile on her face, but she could not help casting a fearful glance toward the kitchen. She gulped slightly, but she had to go on, making the best of things. Tess was not going to be happy about this at all.

"Certainly," Monica said, managing to conceal her misgivings. "Veal instead of pheasant, no sage. I will share that with the chef." Monica turned to Andrew. "And for you, sir?"

Monica said a little prayer. Surely Andrew knew what was going on in the kitchen and would order the menu exactly as it was written. What else could he do? Monica knew that he didn't want to risk the wrath of Tess. But Andrew seemed more intent on making Kate feel comfortable, so he followed her lead. Thus, he did not cooperate, much to Monica's chagrin.

"Make that two," said Andrew with a mischievous smile. "I'd much rather have veal than pheasant." He handed the menu back to Monica and hoped that she would not exact too horrible a revenge on him when this assignment was done.

Monica's face fell. Then she forced her smile back in place. "Very good. Thank you."

Monica returned to the head waiter's podium at the door where she put away the menus. She paused there a moment summoning up her courage to go into the kitchen and tell Tess about the small changes in the plan.

But just as she had more or less steeled her nerves to confront Tess with the bad news of the substitutions, something happened that no one— not Tess, not Andrew, and certainly not Monica— could have anticipated. A second customer walked into the restaurant and surveyed the room, a look of great imperiousness on his deeply lined face. He was tall and thin and almost bald, but he carried himself with great hauteur, a slight look of contempt in his eyes, as if he were always beset by little annoyances and irritants that made his life so very difficult.

He was perfectly dressed in what amounted to the uniform of the New York male of the exclusive Upper East Side—an oxford cloth shirt with a knotted rep tie, gray flannels, and a blue blazer. He seemed rich and bossy and was definitely used to getting his way. Monica's heart sank when she saw him. She could feel in her bones that this man was going to be trouble. There was nothing she would have rather done than get rid of him, but she knew that he would not go easily.

"Excuse me, sir," said Monica diffidently. "May I help you this evening?"

"Is this a restaurant?" the man demanded. His words were clipped and forceful and he had a slight accent—perhaps an English accent or a refined Scottish one. The man glanced around the room, looking hard at Andrew and Kate.

Monica hesitated. "Well . . ." This was the one thing they had not counted on: other diners, even some degree of popularity. What if more people started coming in?

"It is a restaurant," Monica conceded. "But we're terribly new, sir. I'm not sure you'd be happy dining here this evening. Some other time, perhaps. When we've worked out all the kinks and problems." Monica smiled what she hoped was her most winning smile. It would be hard enough on Tess to deal with the substitutions that Monica had offered so rashly. To add an additional customer . . . Well, Monica had no idea how Tess would react to that!

And yet, this formidable man looked unconvinced, completely unmoved by her impassioned plea.

"And this *is* a restaurant?" he asked again.

"Well . . . yes," said Monica. "We've only just opened," she added, "and I'm not at all sure that we'll be able to satisfy a demanding customer such as yourself, sir."

"I am not at all demanding," the man said. "I am merely hungry. Do you understand that?"

"Yes, sir," said Monica.

"And this *is* a restaurant?"

Monica tried to buy a bit of time. "How do you mean, sir? A restaurant?"

This rather grand man did not deem it beneath his dignity to define what he meant by a restaurant. "Tell me, do people sit down at tables here, look at menus and order food and then eat and then get up to leave? Does that happen here, young lady?"

"Well, that's the plan so far," Monica stammered. "But we're not quite set up for anything too—"

The man cut her off. "Then *this is* a restaurant," he said dryly. "And given that it is a restaurant and that it is open to the general public, I wish to have a table, and I demand to be served. And is that clear to you, young lady?"

"Oh, yes," said Monica. "Quite clear." But she did not budge from behind the bulwark of the maître d's desk.

"Then seat me," the man ordered. "And let's hurry up with it, shall we? I'm hungry."

Monica had only one fallback position and she knew it wasn't a terribly good one. "Yes . . . I see . . . ," she said. Monica looked down at the desk top, as if examining notes of great importance. "Would you mind, sir, if I asked you," she said, "if you have a reservation with us this evening?"

The man looked her square in the eye. It was obvious to Monica that he had been faced with this particular gambit before. "Do I have a reservation, you ask? No, I don't. I do not have a reservation. No, sorry about that."

Monica felt relief flood through her. "Well, sir," she said, "without a reservation I'm afraid we couldn't possibly seat you. Not this evening, anyway. So sorry about that, sir." Monica shrugged as if there were nothing more to say.

The man surveyed the restaurant. There were a dozen tables, and only one was occupied, the best table, the one in the corner where an attractive couple was sitting.

"May I ask you a question?" the man said.

"Of course. You may ask me anything."

"You seem to have a very strict policy about reservations," said the man, looking down at the lectern Monica stood behind.

"Oh, yes we do," Monica replied. "The chef insists on it."

"Well," the man asked, "do you have such a thing as a reservation list?"

Monica blanched and did her best to avoid the man's gaze. Well, she was forced to admit he had her there, they had made no provision for a reservation book or list.

"A list," she said. "Um . . . no. There is no list. I mean, we don't have a list now . . . but we are sure to get one sometime in the future. I should think . . ."

"But you choose not to admit me now?" the man asked, sounding quite irate about the state of things. He looked like the type of man who might file a lawsuit if he didn't get exactly what he wanted.

"Well, you know," said Monica, "we've just opened, and we don't want to tax the kitchen all that much. Surely you can see the point of that, sir."

The man surveyed the room, his eyes fixing on Kate and Andrew.

"There are only two diners in this entire restaurant," he protested vehemently. "Preparing dinner for one more will not, I'm sure, overwhelm your chef. And if it does then he has no business in a commercial kitchen."

"That would be *she*, actually," said Monica.

"She, he, what difference does it make?" the man said with a dismissive shrug. "She should be able to manage one more diner, I should think."

Monica could see that this rather demanding patron might have a point. To put him off any more would only create a commotion. Neither Andrew nor Monica wanted that.

"Seat me, please," said the man.

"But of course," Monica replied. "Please follow me, sir."

Monica walked into the dining room, the man following in her wake. She tried to seat him as far away from Andrew and Kate as she dared, but he would have none of it. Without prompting, he chose a table quite close to that of Kate and Andrew. He settled in his chair, grabbed the thick linen napkin, fluffed it, and placed it on his lap.

Andrew looked up in disbelief as he saw Monica lead the elderly man across the restaurant, and she responded to his inquiring glance with a look of helplessness. But all she could do was act as if nothing out of the ordinary were going on. She seated her new customer and handed him the menu, hoping against hope that he would find nothing he wanted to eat written out there.

"Here we go, sir," she said. "We have a fixed menu. This is what our chef will be serving this evening." The elderly man paid little attention to her but scanned the menu intently, like a scholar studying some newly discovered ancient text.

"And may I interest you in something to drink, sir?" Monica asked quietly.

He did not look up from the menu. "I would

like to see the wine list," the man said. "And quickly, if you please."

"Of course, sir," Monica replied.

But the elderly man still did not look up, which was just as well, because the look on Monica's face suggested that the wine list at Chez Tess was just as tangible as its reservation list.

"The wine list," said Monica. "Ah . . . of course . . ." She backed away from this lordly old man as if leaving the presence of royalty. The evening was getting out of hand, but only Monica knew just how irregular things had become. And to top it off, Kate was about to throw a very volatile ingredient into the pot.

As Monica passed, Kate waved, summoning her to the table. She gestured that Monica lower her head so she could whisper in her ear. Kate looked excited—excited the way New Yorkers can be when they have some inside information.

"You do know who that is, don't you?" Kate murmured, pointing at the newly arrived diner. She need not have been so discreet—the man was paying no attention to anything or anyone— in fact, his eyes had still not left the menu.

Monica exchanged a quick glance with Andrew. "No, I don't," she said. "He didn't have a reservation, so I don't know his name. Should I know him?"

"Well, he wouldn't have given his real name anyway," said Kate. "The critics never do. And yes, you should know who he is. He's a star in New York food circles."

"The critics?" asked Monica.

"That man is Norman Delmonico," Kate announced triumphantly, as if this piece of information would definitely get a rise out of Monica.

"And who is Norman Delmonico?" Monica asked.

"You have a restaurant in New York and you've never heard of Norman Delmonico?" said Kate. "He is *the* food critic."

"He is?" said Monica, feeling a little foolish.

"That's right," said Kate urgently. "And you had better let your chef know that he's here."

"Why?" Monica asked.

Kate looked at Monica as if she had lost her mind. "Why? Because a good review from him and you're made—a bad review and you are out of business. Everybody reads him, and there aren't a lot of people who dare to disagree with him. *That's* why."

Monica did not know that a certain level of New York City society followed the opening and closing of first-class restaurants, tracked which restaurants were in and which were out, the way sports fans lived and died with their teams.

Certain chefs at certain New York restaurants were celebrities. Food critics wielded immense power. Some of them worked hard to preserve their anonymity and insisted that they never be photographed—certain restaurants were known to pay bounties for tips on forthcoming visits by influential critics. But Norman Delmonico was far from anonymous. Quite the contrary, he was something of a New York fixture, a well-known member of the culture corps, one of the opinion makers who wrote the influential columns in newspapers and magazines, telling New Yorkers exactly what to think.

His face was well-known to just about everybody. Delmonico did not mind being photographed for the society columns; he could be seen on television pontificating about food and wine, and he and his photograph sat atop his column.

"I see," said Monica. As far as she knew, Chez Tess was going to be in business for one night only and serve exactly three meals—one more than planned—so reviews were not something she had given any thought to. On the other hand, she did have to keep up the facade.

"Oh, yes. I'll take care of that, and I know the chef will be so grateful. Thanks for spotting him, Dr. Calder." Monica hurried away as if anxious to give the chef all the good news.

Tess was happy in the kitchen. She was dressed in chef's whites with a giant toque perched on her head, and she sang as she moved from pot to pot as they bubbled on top of a big, professional range.

"I'm cooking, I'm cooking," she sang, "with a blessing, with a blessing for *evvvverrry-one!*"

MY DINNER *with* ANDREW

The pheasant was slow-roasting in the oven,
the *salade nicoise* with ahi had already been
arranged in the vertical heap that a lot of New
York restaurants affected with appetizers. The
reduction was reducing. All in all, considering
the haste with which Chez Tess had been assembled, things could not have been going better in
the kitchen.

As Monica swept into the kitchen, Tess handed
her a basket of crusty, fragrant, fresh-baked bread
that had just come out of the oven.

"How's it going out there?" Tess asked as
she put curls of sweet butter on a small plate.
She paused a moment and looked at the butter.
"Should we serve butter or be really chic and
trendy and send out a dish of extra virgin olive
oil instead?"

"How about both?" suggested Monica.

"Sure, why not?" said Tess. "They're both
good. So, how is it going out there? Angel Boy
doing his job?"

"Andrew is doing fine," Monica replied evenly.
Then she took a deep breath, finally able to give
Tess the bad news. "However, . . ."

Tess looked up. "However? However, what? I never like sentences that begin with 'however.'"

"However, there have been a couple of substitution requests," Monica said, hoping she sounded nonchalant. "Nothing to be worried about, really."

Tess' eyebrows arched, and she gazed balefully at Monica. "Oh, really," she said. "Substitutions? And who, may I ask, told Kate and Andrew that substitutions were allowed?" The question was purely rhetorical, of course; Tess knew that Monica was prone to giving in to her own enthusiasm in the excitement of the moment.

"Well," said Monica gingerly, "purely in the spirit of hospitality . . . I did. It seemed like the right thing to do. And that Dr. Calder knows her own mind."

"You did?" said Tess, a little miffed that her well-run kitchen was being disturbed. "And just how hospitable are we going to be?"

Consulting her order pad, Monica replied, "They would like veal instead of the pheasant, no sage in the lemon reduction," she announced.

"And tea instead of coffee." She held up two fingers. "And that would be twice."

"I haven't added the sage to the reduction yet," grumbled Tess. "And tea instead of coffee is easy. But no *pheasant*? The pheasant is . . . it's a masterpiece, Monica. A masterpiece. I do all this cooking, and no one is going to have it?"

Monica shook her head slowly. "No pheasant, Tess. Well, at least, not at table one . . ." She took the basket of bread and made her escape, returning to the relative peace of the dining room. Monica was very relieved. Tess had handled the news of the substitutions much better than she had expected.

Tess gaped as Monica swept out. "Table one? If there's a table one," she said, "that would suggest that there is a table two . . ."

Chapter Seven

There was no champagne or rich food on the menu for Beth Popik that evening. She had worked as late as she could, then left the lab to go home. Since she did not live in the city, she could not stay as late at Nichols BioTech as she would have liked, but was ruled, instead, by the tyranny of the train schedule. The last train to her suburban home north of the city left Grand Central Station at 7:06, and Beth knew from experience that she had to leave work at least twenty minutes before that to catch the train, arriving at the station just as the doors of the train were about to close. She *never* got there in time to get a seat.

Just over an hour after leaving Grand Central Station she arrived at her modest little house. It had been built before the suburb grew up around it, so Beth's home had a little more character than the suburban split-levels that surrounded it. She always loved getting home, closing her front door on the pressures and tribulations of the day. Most soothing of all, though, was the warm welcome she got from her dog—a big, shaggy mongrel called Bruno. He was an old dog, so when she came home Bruno didn't go into a frenzy of barking as a puppy might, but he would lick her hand and look genuinely glad to have her back.

From that moment on Beth could more or less predict every minute of the rest of the evening; her routine rarely varied. She would prepare dinner for herself and her dog, she would bathe, and then, dressed for bed, she would settle on the couch, a pile of reading material in her lap— mostly articles from scientific journals. She would have the television set on, but more to break the silence than anything else.

That evening there were two slight variations

in her regular procedure. She lit a fire in the fireplace against the unseasonable spring chill, and she found herself thinking about Kate Calder and her date with Dr. Andrew Friend. The image of the handsome young man was in her mind's eye when she began to feel unaccountably sleepy . . .

Kate had let her guard down, just about as low as it would go. She and Andrew were deep in conversation—and for once she wasn't analyzing and testing every word he said; she wasn't suspicious. She was relaxed, and she was having a good time, so much so that she hadn't even noticed Andrew's subtle approach. She appeared to be at ease—an unusual state for Dr. Katherine Calder.

Monica had served their first course, the pile of salad with the grilled ahi tuna, crusted on the outside, pink on the inside, and dribbled with a touch of ginger and wasabi. They continued to drink champagne, a perfect companion to the sharp Japanese mustard and the delicate flavor of the fish and greens. The food was delicious, but as sometimes happens, the conversation became more interesting than the food. They ate, but they hardly noticed the delectable creations on their plates.

"So tell me what it is you do," Andrew said. "Now that you've heard what *I* do."

"You wouldn't understand," she said bluntly.

Andrew refused to be offended. "Try me."

Kate put down her fork. "Do you know anything about DNA polymorphism and genetic maps?"

"Absolutely nothing," said Andrew, laughing.

"How about the phenotypic diversity of mutations occurring in a single gene? Or how about oligonucleotide probing for hybridization of chromosome specificity?"

"You want to put that in layperson's terms, Doctor?" said Andrew.

Kate laughed. "I'm doing genetic research," she said simply. "I'm looking for the structure in a gene that might suggest what diseases a person may be susceptible to."

"Wait a minute," said Andrew, puzzled. "I'm not sure I follow you, Kate."

"It's the hot topic in medicine now," Kate said. "And make no mistake, every doctor engaged in research wants to discover one of these genes."

"You are looking for a *susceptibility* gene?" he said. "Some kind of signpost that's going to point the way to disease?" It sounded to him like science fiction, but it was plainly something that Kate took very seriously.

Kate nodded. "Sure . . . Imagine being able to take a test and find out that you've got a gene in your chromosomes that says you have got a really good chance of getting breast cancer or Alzheimer's or Lou Gehrig's disease—" Kate looked at Andrew with a very steady gaze. "What if science could tell you how you're going to die? Think of what a difference that would make to *life*."

Of course, Kate could not know that she was talking to someone who was very familiar with death. And, needless to say, Andrew chose not to enlighten her—not just yet, anyway.

"You could also turn it around," he said. "Knowing of a gene like that could give you a chance of avoiding that disease, and staving off death for a while."

Kate nodded. "That's right. That's the point exactly. Genetic counseling is going to change the world. Knowledge will be power—the power to control death."

"You can never control death," said Andrew quietly. "Not completely, anyway."

"Well then, to be able to manage it in a way that it has never been managed before," said Kate passionately. "Death may be inevitable, but that doesn't mean we shouldn't put up the best fight we can. That is the knowledge that we're searching for in this project. And we're getting there."

Andrew had no trouble envisioning the downside of Kate's research. "That knowledge . . ." he said. "Something like that could be pretty scary if the wrong people got hold of it."

Kate shrugged off the remark. The implications of the work she did interested her only as they regarded science and research. Sociological consequences were none of her business. When she said she believed in science she meant it. Anything beyond the realm of her research was of little interest to her.

"I'm a scientist," she said simply. "Not a politician, thank goodness."

Then she paused and stopped chewing as if aware for the first time of what she was putting in her mouth. "The food here is fabulous," she said. "Really incredible." She glanced over at Norman Delmonico. "I wonder if he's having as good a meal as we are. If he is, it's going to be quite a glowing review. A real rave."

Andrew was enjoying the food, too, but he was more concerned with Kate and her work. "So," he asked, "what disease are you looking for?"

Kate shook her head, a curt little gesture. "That's not how it works. You see, all the major medical centers have divided up the different chromosomes. We at Nichols have been assigned to study Chromosome Twelve."

"How do you go about doing something like that?" Andrew asked. "And what are you looking for exactly?"

"Everything," said Kate simply. "We examine everything we can about that one chromosome. We're trying to find a pattern—we call it a 'gene sequence'—something that could indicate a tendency toward disease. But we don't know what disease we're looking for, and we don't know where to look. It's like trying to break the combination on a lock, and we don't even know what the safe looks like."

"Speaking of safes," asked Andrew, "what's that big one in your office for? It looked pretty serious."

"Well, there's a lot of competition in medical research," she said matter-of-factly. "It's not unheard of for data to be stolen, faked, plagiarized, or altered."

Andrew feigned surprise. "You? Competitive? *No!* I would never believe it."

Kate laughed heartily and sipped her champagne, her eyes glittering. She found herself beginning to like Andrew, and she was glad that he had insisted that she make good on her six-thousand-dollar date. She was surprised to find that she was having a very good time.

Even though Norman Delmonico was sitting only a yard or two from Kate and Andrew, he did not notice them, paid no attention to them—he did not even hear Kate's unrestrained laughter. Rather, his interest was completely taken up with the bottle of wine that Monica was serving. He sniffed the cork deeply, then watched as she poured a small amount into his glass.

He stuck his nose into the glass, swirled the deep crimson liquid, then sipped. His eyes widened as he swallowed.

"Where in the world did you get this?" Norman was so surprised he could barely get the words out. "Do you know what this is? This is an 1870 Chateau LaTour LaFitte Rothschild."

Monica looked apologetic as she filled his glass. She knew absolutely nothing about wine and her ignorance showed.

"I know . . . It's terribly old, but I'm afraid it was all we could come up with. We're still getting our wine list together. We've only just opened, you know . . ."

"But, but—" Delmonico stammered, "this wine isn't *old*—it's extinct. Finding a drinkable bottle of 1870 LaTour is like finding the Holy Grail. This is absolutely impossible!" In all his years in the food business Norman Delmonico had never seen a bottle of such rare wine—let alone actually tasted the contents. A wine produced and bottled in 1870 should have turned into a bottle of sediment and sludge. But this wine was deep and rich, its body almost flesh and blood. He had never tasted anything quite so exquisite.

"Astonishing," Norman exclaimed. "Absolutely astonishing. But unbelievable—no one is going to believe this. It's impossible!"

Monica smiled sweetly. "Well, you see, sir, the owner of this restaurant tends to specialize in the impossible. Bon appétit!" She withdrew to the kitchen, leaving Norman Delmonico, a man not easy to surprise, in something of a state of shock.

Tess was cooking up a storm, moving from pot to pot, mixing, stirring, sprinkling spices like stardust.

"A food critic!" she grumbled. "Of all the people in the world to walk in right off the street . . . I don't mind surprises, I don't mind the cooking. I don't even mind substitutions. But what I do not like is a critic." She looked at Monica, her eyes blazing.

"That poor man," said Monica. "I'm just a little bit worried about him."

"Him?" snorted Tess angrily. "All critics ever do is tear down other people's work. And I'm the one under pressure here. Why feel sorry for him?"

Monica shrugged. "Don't you see, Tess . . . he's probably going to write a review—most likely a great review—of a restaurant that won't be here tomorrow morning."

"So?" said Tess.

"Today he is the most powerful restaurant critic in all of New York City, or so Kate Calder says," said Monica. "And when that review comes out tomorrow . . . well, what's that going to do to his credibility? It might destroy him."

Tess waved away Monica's worries. "That's exactly how people get into trouble, worrying about tomorrow. You want to worry about something, worry about my lemon reduction, Miss Wings . . ."

Chapter Eight

*A*ndrew and Kate sat at their table as oblivious to Norman Delmonico as he was to them. Delmonico was still confounded and nonplussed by the exceptional food and wine he had found at this unknown restaurant; similarly, Andrew and Kate were so caught up in their conversation it was as if they had managed to close out the rest of the world.

"I don't understand," Andrew persisted. "It seems to me, the more information that scientists share with one another, the sooner they can discover cures for things, and eradicate disease." He sat back in his chair and sipped his champagne.

Kate shook her head. "Medicine is competitive because medicine is business, just like everything else" she said vehemently. "If you don't get there first, you don't get the jobs or the grants or the fame or whatever else you want. There's a bottom line in medicine and for most people it is money. Lots of it. Do you know how much money is made each year in this country off diabetes? Or asthma—or even the common cold? The figures are immense."

Andrew stared at her for a moment. "You're not interested in money," he said. "I can tell." And that interested Andrew. He knew it was a rare trait to find in a modern human being—a lack of interest in material things—but Kate Calder plainly did not care about any of the tangible rewards of her profession.

Kate's eyes flashed. "You're right. I'm not."

"So what is it you want then?"

"Immortality," said Kate bluntly.

Andrew laughed lightly. "I have a couple of suggestions for that," he said. "You might want to hear them sometime. I am something of an expert on immortality."

Kate smiled wryly. "And let me guess; your suggestions probably have something to do with heaven, right?" She shook her head slowly. "Heaven . . . ," she said.

"It has a *lot* to do with it, actually," said Andrew. "But you knew that, right?"

"I'm not making fun of you," said Kate, a note of apology creeping into her voice. "It's just that heaven is not part of my vocabulary. I'm only interested in what I can prove. And if I can discover something no one else has and prove it, then I'll make it into the history books. And that is important to me. It means a lot to me, and nothing will change that."

"Why is that so important to you?" Andrew asked. "Why does that drive you?"

Kate shrugged. "That, in my opinion, is the only thing that will allow me to live forever."

"But I *still* don't understand why that is so important." Andrew had never known someone so young to be so concerned about how she would be remembered after death. It was very peculiar. "I don't get it, Kate. Why?"

Kate hesitated a moment. Hardly anyone

knew her secret, yet something made her want to confide in Andrew. She said, "Because I'm dying."

Andrew stared at her. "That can't be true," he said. And he *knew* that it couldn't be true.

But Kate thought his denial was nothing more than the usual reflexive gainsaying, that it was mere rhetoric on his part.

"I've got cancer," she said matter-of-factly. "It's a form of leukemia. It's going to kill me some day, but right now I'm still here, still very much alive." She flashed him a little smile. "And that's thanks to science, by the way. I'm the subject of an experimental treatment program—so experimental that nobody can say how long I've got. So, you see, I understand the value of knowing what you're going to die of."

"How long?" Andrew asked. "How much time do your doctors say you might have left?"

There was another shrug from Kate. "Five, maybe even six years." She laughed and shook her head. "That's not a long time, but I'm hoping that it will be sufficient for me. I've got work to do and do not intend to be denied it. I only hope it will be time enough to finish my work."

"I'm sure it will be, Kate," said Andrew.

She laughed again, shaking her head ruefully. "I know you think I'm some pushy broad who just has to be first in line and win the auction and beat the other kids and keep all my secrets to myself."

She leaned forward and gripped the table tightly. Suddenly it was very important to her that Andrew understand her point of view, that he realize that what appeared to be mere self-ishness was in fact a type of self-preservation.

"But discovering a new gene, Andrew, that could change the world, doing that on my own, making a name for myself, that's all I have to live for now. And it's the only thing that'll be left when I go, the difference that I made in this world." She was looking deep into his eyes now, begging him to try to understand every word she had said.

And she did get through to him. Andrew found that he was deeply moved—for the very first time he had seen beyond Kate's carefully

constructed facade and had caught a glimpse of
her as a real and very vulnerable person. Without
thinking, he reached out and took her hand in
his, squeezing it lightly. She did not pull back,
did not snatch her hand away. But before he
could speak, Monica approached the table.

"Excuse me, sir," she said softly but earnestly.
"I believe you have a call at the front desk."

Andrew and Kate had been caught up in the
moment and Monica's words cut into it. "Oh,"
he said. He let go of Kate's hand and looked
around the room as if seeing it for the first time.
"A call? Really?" He looked very puzzled.

Then he looked past Kate and saw that Adam
had arrived in the restaurant, and it was clear that
they had to confer.

"I'm sorry," Andrew said to Kate apologet-
ically. "I have to take this . . . excuse me."

Andrew stood and followed Monica, joining
Adam at the door of the restaurant. "How's it
going?" Adam asked. "I'm sorry I wasn't here
sooner."

"Well," said Andrew with a little shrug of his
shoulders, "I'm finally getting a clue as to what

we're all doing here. She's dying. And she knows it."

Monica's eyes grew wide. "What?" she gasped.

Andrew nodded. "Yeah, that's right, she's dying. But she doesn't need me. Not yet."

He glanced over his shoulder quickly. "This lady's got to get her priorities straight. At least her doctor said she has some time left—five or six years. She's completely obsessed with making a significant medical breakthrough, a discovery—something that she can leave behind after she dies. She has no conception of an afterlife—or a here and now, for that matter. She runs roughshod over her colleagues and her life is completely consumed by her research work. She pays no attention at all to her spiritual life." Andrew sighed heavily. "That's got to change. She needs someone like you, Monica."

"Me?" said Monica. "But you said she's dying."

"She has a few years," Andrew replied. "And she's got to be taught to use those next few years very wisely. If she's got five years, then she has time, I'd say. A lot can happen in five years."

"That's time enough," Monica agreed.

But something was plainly bothering Adam. "Five years?" he said. "She's not going to die in five years."

"Well, maybe not exactly five years, but she has a good bit of time to get her house in order."

"No, no," Adam insisted. "Understand that we aren't talking years here, Andrew."

"We're not?" Andrew said.

"No," Adam replied. "That woman over there is going to die tonight."

Andrew and Monica stared at Adam, shock plain on their faces. Then they looked back at Kate, who sat unaware, her champagne glass light in her hand. She was staring out the window at the glittering lights of the office towers and the great yellow moon and the cold stars that seemed to hang in the night sky. She was happier in that moment than she could remember being in a long time and she was, for a change, at peace.

Chapter Nine

The angels gathered in the kitchen for a hurried conference on the subject of Dr. Kate Calder. On one hand, it was simply too hard for Monica, Tess, and Andrew to believe that Kate's time had come; on the other, they knew that Adam got his information on High Authority.

"She looks perfectly normal, Adam," Monica protested. "What do you mean she's going to die tonight? Are you sure?"

"Well, she has a disease," said Andrew. "It's fatal, but it's slow. She said she had at least five years."

Adam was matter-of-fact, almost to the point

of flippancy. "Well she's not going to die of that disease tonight," he said. "It will be something else. A car accident, a stroke, a chandelier could fall on her head—"

"Oh hush, Adam," said Tess.

Adam shrugged. "I don't know how she's going to die," he said. "All I know is I was supposed to be there when it happened. It's standard procedure—all of you know that."

Andrew nodded. "And now I'm the one who has to be there," he said. It was an assignment he was looking forward to fulfilling.

But Monica was still full of questions. "Out of all the men in that auction, what made her bid on an angel?" She looked around the room. "Any ideas?"

"Sometimes, when death is near, people get a sense of it," Tess said gently. "I suppose God knew that, given the chance, she would want an angel with her today, whether she knew why or not."

"I don't know . . ." Andrew sounded far from convinced. "This lady is not the angel type, Tess." He had been on enough assignments to know the type who needed an angel and those who didn't. Kate Calder definitely fell into the latter category. If he was going to get through to her before it was too late—by the end of that very evening—he knew he had his work cut out for him.

But Tess was not convinced by Andrew's intuition. "Maybe she knows that," she replied. "Maybe deep down inside she wants to change that part of her before it's too late." She shrugged. She knew from experience that you could never quite read the map of the human mind, that human beings had an astonishing ability to change their minds in a split second.

Andrew shook his head slowly. He refused to be convinced. "I don't know, Tess. That lady is an awfully tough case. One of the toughest I've ever encountered. She's thought about death and life, and she's made up her mind."

"Maybe she just seems tough, Andrew," Tess replied. "Sometimes it's those hard types who see the light faster and sooner than the ones who never give the big questions a second thought."

"Well, it's later than she thinks. A lot later,"

said Adam. "Monica, you may want to serve dessert with the entrée," he said teasingly.

Monica was shocked that Adam could make light of such a solemn situation. She snapped at him with a dish towel. "You never change, you know that, Adam?"

Adam threw his arm up to protect himself. "Sorry, Monica—I'm too old to change." Then he turned to Andrew. "Look, I'm really sorry you're in this position, Andrew. It ought to be me out there, not you. If there's anything I can do to help you out, just let me know."

Before Andrew could answer, Tess stepped up, tossing an apron at him. "Yeah," she barked. "Put this on and stir!"

"Yes, ma'am," said Adam meekly.

Andrew made for the door, Monica at his side. "I can't believe it," he said with a shake of his head. "This doesn't feel right. It feels too soon for her to go."

"Be very careful, Andrew," Monica cautioned. "Remember to heed the advice that you're always giving me: don't get too emotionally involved with your charges."

"I'm not getting too involved," said Andrew. "Really, I'm not." And he might have genuinely believed that—but no one else in that kitchen did.

Andrew hurried back to his table, feeling that he had been a very bad host and had left his guest alone for far too long. But Kate seemed unaware of his long absence and was sitting at the table, calm and composed, when he returned.

"Is everything okay?" Kate asked.

"Oh, yes," he said. He cocked an ear and listened to the piano for a moment or two, then extended his hand. "Would you care to dance, Kate?"

Kate hesitated a moment, then, beaming, took his hand and allowed herself to be guided onto the dance floor. They began to sway to the music, the two of them falling into the rhythm of the song. Kate was a graceful dancer, and Andrew was pretty light on his feet. She was impressed with his skill.

"If I believed in God," said Kate, "which I don't, I'd say this place was as close to heaven as I could get. I hope that doesn't give you any ideas."

Andrew smiled slyly. "Just one—heaven," he said. "Funny you should bring that up. Play along with me for a minute. It won't take long. Don't worry."

"Uh-oh," said Kate. "I think I feel a sermon coming on. The big push from God's representative."

"No," said Andrew, laughing lightly. "No sermon, I promise. But think about what you just said—people live and people die. What do you think happens after that, Kate?"

"Nothing," she replied bluntly. Then she added with a shrug, "Decomposition. Probate. People grieve. They've just discovered that grief is something that never passes. Did you know that? It used to be that people thought it was something that passed, that scabbed over and eventually went away. And if that didn't happen you were likely to have someone tell you to 'put it behind you,' or 'get over it, already.' But researchers have found that you carry grief with you until *you* die."

"And then the cycle starts all over again, with the loved ones you've left behind," said Andrew.

Kate smiled wanly. "The cycle can be broken. I don't imagine I'm going to get much in the way of grief. But that's just fine with me. I don't want it."

"What do you want?" Andrew asked.

"I told you. I hope to have a plaque somewhere with my name on it. That's it, Andrew. The rest is wishful thinking. You die and what? You 'go to heaven.' There's no proof of heaven. So how can you be so sure of going there?" She finished her statement with the air of a prosecutor who had delivered a stunning blow to the case for the defense.

But Andrew had run into this argument before, and he countered without much effort. "Oh, that's easy," he said with a smile. "It's been done."

Kate laughed tolerantly. "Okay, let's assume that I die, and I go to heaven. Then what? I float around like some kind of bliss-filled amoeba with no food, no champagne, no cable TV. That doesn't sound like anyone's idea of heaven, Andrew. I mean, let's face it, who wants to live forever like that?"

"I couldn't agree more," said Andrew. "Nobody wants to live like that, and God would not ask you to. It's funny. If I asked you what hell was like, you'd know in a minute—people have a much clearer idea of what hell is like than heaven."

"Right. That's because deep down I think we're all sure there's a hell but can't believe there's a heaven. And a lot of us are *sure* we are headed to hell." Kate sounded serious. "There must be a reason that painters have painted pictures of hell over the centuries. I can't recall a single painting of heaven."

"It doesn't have to be that way," said Andrew. "But I *can't* paint you a picture. I can't draw to save my life."

Kate smiled. "No? Okay then, why don't you *tell* me something about heaven?"

"Anything," Andrew replied. "Ask me anything."

"So how many cable channels *has* He got?" She stopped dancing dead in the middle of the floor. "'Cause if He hasn't got cable, I'm not going near the place. Understood?"

Andrew laughed and led her from the dance floor, the two of them taking stools at the intimate little bar at Chez Tess.

"You are really something," he said, shaking his head. "Really something." He gazed at her for a moment. "Okay . . ." He paused for a moment. "Okay. I want you to imagine you're locked in a closet. For years."

Kate smiled broadly. "I know all about that. You're talking about my laboratory. Much as I love my work, sometimes that lab feels as confining as a prison cell."

Andrew ignored the joke and plunged on. "And it turns out that during this incarceration, you give birth to a baby."

"I do?"

Andrew nodded. "Yes, you do."

"This is getting very weird," Kate said. "Any idea who the father might be?"

"It doesn't matter," said Andrew. He refused

153

to be pushed off the topic at hand. "Stick with me here. You don't know if you're ever going to get out, but you hope so. In the meantime, you draw little pictures of dogs and trees and birds. You do this to show your baby, who has never seen any of it, what life is like out in the real world."

Kate nodded slowly. "Okay . . ."

"And then one day," Andrew continued, "the baby comes to you and says something like 'Gee, trees and dogs and birds and houses in the real world are pretty small and flat, aren't they, Mom?'"

The look on Andrew's face intensified, and his eyes seemed to become an even deeper shade of blue. "And that's when you realize that no matter how hard you try to draw the picture, you'll never be able to get that baby of yours to imagine what reality looks like. Not until he sees it for himself. So until then, you tell your child you love him, and you ask him to trust you."

Andrew paused to let the full weight of his words sink in. They were staring at each other, their eyes locked together. The only sound in the room was the tinkling of the piano keys.

"So," said Kate after a while, "you're telling me that heaven is the ultimate reality, huh? Is that what you tell your dying patients? How do they react to that?"

"No," Andrew replied. "I don't tell them that. That's what I *share* with them. Because I go through it with them." His face was still and solemn.

Kate's eyes had not left his face. "I've never met anyone like you before," she said. "You really believe this—you *really* believe in God—but you're not one of those angry, pushy types. You know the kind of person I mean."

Andrew knew where she was going, but he refused to pass judgment on anyone or their beliefs. "God makes Himself known to everyone in His own way, Kate," he said gently.

"See," she said. "That's what I mean about you. You are so . . . understanding."

As she spoke her face seemed to soften, and her eyes grew misty.

"You remind me of . . . I don't know . . ." Her cheeks colored as she flushed with embarrassment. "I know this isn't going to come out right." She paused another moment or two, as if summoning up the courage to speak her heart. "You look like . . . love."

She laughed and looked away, feeling silly and self-conscious at such a naked display of emotion. In that moment not one of her colleagues at the laboratory would have recognized her as the stern and severe Dr. Kate Calder.

Andrew took her by the hand. "That is the most wonderful thing that anyone has ever said to me." Then he lowered his lips to her hand and kissed it lightly before leading her back to the dance floor.

Standing in the doorway of her kitchen, Tess saw the kiss and was not pleased. She really disliked it when one of her angels became emotionally involved in a case—and yet angels were naturally compassionate, so *not* getting involved was very difficult. Still, Tess did not like it.

"What *is* it with that boy?" she said aloud.

Behind her, Adam was slaving over a hot stove. He opened his mouth to answer her question (Adam always had an opinion on any subject you could care to name and he was not afraid to give it), but Tess stopped him. She stepped back into the kitchen and waved a threatening finger at the angel.

"I don't need to hear from you," she snapped. "You just keep stirring!"

Chapter Ten

*W*hen Tess stepped out of the kitchen a moment or two after yelling at Adam, her chef's hat and kitchen uniform whites were gone. Now she was wearing a simple but elegant black evening gown under a dramatic red opera jacket. It was brightly decorated with shimmering spangles and sequins. No one who saw her then would have guessed that this well-dressed woman had been, just moments before, dressed in work clothes and laboring over the hot grill in the restaurant kitchen.

Monica saw her emerge in her finery but said nothing. Whatever Tess was up to would be sure to manifest itself shortly. Monica was more concerned about Norman Delmonico. Ever since taking his first sip of that rarest of wines, the 1870 Chateau LaFitte, he had not been able to slake his appetite.

Contrary to popular belief, restaurant critics are not gluttons—they can't afford to be. They eat in fine restaurants almost every night of the year, and despite any enthusiasm they have for their jobs, they have to pace themselves, to rein in their desires or risk jading the palate completely.

Typically, a restaurant critic like Norman dined in the company of at least two or three friends. He would taste food from their plates as well as his own, and he might return to the restaurant three or four times before filing a review.

But this night was different—and the food at Chez Tess was decidedly unusual. In fact, it was completely out of the realm of anything he had ever experienced. The food was so good that the normally restrained Norman Delmonico was unable to control himself. From the first taste of the first piece of bread, he had fallen victim to the exquisite—the *heavenly*—flavors of Tess' cooking. They had overwhelmed him, washing away any reserve, consuming him in a fever of pure, mad immoderation. He had worked his way through the prix fixe menu in an ecstatic feeding frenzy, eating with both hands, cramming the food into his mouth as if he hadn't tasted nourishment in six months or more.

The sight disconcerted Monica, and while she knew the maxim about the customer always being right, she felt obliged to say something to him. She approached the arrogant food critic with some trepidation.

"Excuse me, sir," she said softly, not wanting to scare him. Delmonico had his face down close to the plate like a dog—Monica half expected him to growl if she got too close to his dinner. "I hope you don't mind me saying so, sir, but you really shouldn't eat so quickly. There's plenty more where that came from. Really there is. Take it slowly, please, sir."

Delmonico looked up but didn't stop chewing. "I can't help it," he said, his voice filled with bliss. "This isn't food," he declared. "This is life itself. I have never eaten—never experienced *anything* like this, not here in New York, not in Europe, not the Far East. The chef is a genius—"

"Oh, yes," Monica agreed, "she is that."

"The textures, the aroma," Delmonico raved on, "the indescribable fluidity of flavors. It's the most astonishing meal of my life. This is the finest restaurant in the city—never mind the city, there's probably no better place anywhere in the world."

He looked up at Monica, gazing at her beseechingly. "I must have more, young lady. What else have you got back there?" He peered over at the table where Kate and Andrew had been sitting. "What did those people have?"

"They had veal, sir," said Monica.

"I didn't see veal on the menu."

"It was a substitution," said Monica sheepishly. "Made in the spirit of hospitality, you understand."

"Then be as hospitable to me, young lady," Delmonico ordered. "Bring me the veal as well."

"Yes, sir," said Monica, withdrawing quickly, leaving Delmonico to his delirious, gluttonous rapture.

Tess was aware of the situation with Delmonico, but she had to leave that in Monica's hands. She was more concerned with Andrew's predicament—that's why she had emerged from the kitchen. Decked out in her finery, she marched into the restaurant, striding past the food critic, crossing the dance floor—she ignored Andrew and Kate, the two of them still dancing and talking—making straight for the piano.

The rather pallid dance music that was dribbling out of the instrument did not suit her purposes at all. She gave the baby grand a purposeful, swift kick and instantly the music changed, shifting from the ambling, rhythmic tinkling to a more forceful arpeggio, and then into the introductory bars of a song.

Tess knew that she had to send a message to Andrew, and there is no better way to get your point across in a situation like this than through a song. Singing in her rich, deep, smoky voice, Tess launched into the old Bergman/Legrand standard—an old song, but one with lyrics fresh and fitting to the situation at hand.

"*What are you doing the rest of your life,*" Tess

sang slowly and soulfully. "*North and South and East and West of your life. . . I have only one request of your life, that you spend it all with me.*"

Andrew and Kate continued to dance. If she heard the lyrics of the song, she gave no indication. Her eyes were closed, her cheek was resting on his shoulder, and the look on her face suggested that while her body was in the restaurant, her mind was somewhere far, far away.

"*All the seasons and times of your days, all the nickels and dimes of your days,*" Tess sang on. "*Let the reasons and rhymes of your days all begin and end with me.*"

Just as Tess intended, Andrew got the message. With Kate still in his arms, the two of them moving slowly on the dance floor, Andrew picked up the thread of the conversation.

"So," he said, "let's say you didn't have five years to live. What would you do if you only had one night left to live?"

Kate opened her eyes, as if awakening from a dream. She laughed at Andrew's question. "Life and death . . . ," she said. "There seems to be a theme to this evening. It's hard to imagine having such a good time with this subject coming up over and over again."

"Come on," said Andrew. "Tell me what you would do if this were your last night on earth."

Kate laughed again. "Oh well," she said, "that's an easy one. "If this were my last night on earth there is only one thing I could do."

"And that is?" Andrew asked.

"I think I'd have to kill myself," Kate said tartly. "There would be nothing else for me to do."

Andrew frowned. There was, he knew, no greater waste of life and emotion than to give in to despair. Suicide was the ultimate act of despair, the final insult against hope.

"Why?" he asked.

Kate smiled mischievously. "Can you keep a secret?"

"Try me."

"I've done it," Kate said. The triumph and jubilation in her voice were plain. "I have found a gene sequence. I really found one."

Tess continued to sing. "*I want to see your*

face, in every kind of light, in fields of gold and forests of the night . . ."

Andrew shared her joy, even if he wasn't quite sure what she had achieved. She looked so plainly happy that he could not help but feel the bliss radiating from her face. "So you've discovered a gene for a disease?"

"Almost," Kate replied. "It's like finding the map. All I have to do now is let it lead me to the treasure. It's just a matter of time. But I'm just about there. Finally, after all this time . . ." Kate shrugged. "So if I died tonight without seeing my work through to its completion, I would be devastated. Wouldn't you be?"

Andrew nodded. "I can understand that, I guess. But I don't like talk about suicide. You should never give in to despair and hopelessness, you know."

"I'll try not to . . . at least not until my work is done. That's the most important thing. That's all I can focus on."

"And when you stand before the candles on a cake, oh let me be the one to hear the silent wish

that you make." Tess brought the song to a soft, gentle close.

Kate's statements evoked a series of complicated emotions in Andrew. She needed a little time, not the five or six years she thought she had; maybe just a matter of weeks, perhaps even days. But no angel, not even the Angel of Death, had power over life and death. If he had some kind of power, Andrew would be loathe to use it, even to grant this small wish that could lead to such a great discovery. He knew that God did not make mistakes, though His plan did not always seem clear to angels or humans.

"How much time do you need?" Andrew asked. "How long would it take to follow your map to the treasure?"

"A few weeks," said Kate. "Maybe a month, perhaps two. That's why I'm so big on security these days."

"Why? What difference does it make?"

Kate laughed again. "What difference does it make? Andrew, it makes all the difference in the world."

"How so?"

"Don't be so naive," Kate retorted. "If somebody got hold of those notes now . . . somebody like Beth, she could claim the work as her own. It wouldn't take her much time at all to use my work to identify the gene and take all the credit for herself."

"How much time would it take if you and Beth worked together?" Andrew asked gently.

The joy faded in Kate's face and a coldness came into her eyes. "You don't get it, do you? If we worked together, we would share the credit. That just is not an option, Andrew. Don't you understand?"

She could feel her anger building like a head of steam. She had been so happy a moment ago that it made her fury more intense. There was a bitter taste in her mouth and she seemed to spit out her words.

"I'm sorry, Andrew," she said caustically. "I know it doesn't sound very religious or heavenly, but I *want* the credit. I've worked for it. I deserve it. It's mine." She broke from the embrace and turned her back to him. "I wish I hadn't told you," she said. "I really wish I hadn't. I think I'd better be going now."

"I'll see you home," said Andrew hurriedly. He knew he had to spend more time with her. There were things she had to work out this very night before it was time to take her to her *real* home.

Kate stopped him. "No," she said coldly. "Remember our deal? I arrive alone. I leave alone."

She stalked back toward the table, intending to grab her purse and leave. It was plain that the evening was over—and it had ended in the disappointment and mortification she had more or less anticipated at the outset.

"Kate," said Andrew as he followed her back to the table, "I have to tell you. I have a secret too."

Oh God, Kate thought, *here it comes. The inevitable.* "Let me guess. You're married, right?"

"No."

"You'd be surprised, you know," said Kate bitterly. "That's the secret I usually get to hear."

She reached the table, picked up her purse, and turned toward the door, ready to leave.

"Please," said Andrew. "At least stay and finish your champagne . . . and hear my secret."

Kate struggled with herself for a moment or two, then permitted her curiosity to overwhelm her anger and her bitterness. She sat down and faced Andrew across the table like a hostile witness. For Kate the magic had gone out of the evening. Suddenly, she looked tired and depressed.

"Okay," she said wearily. "Tell me."

Andrew took a moment to frame his thoughts. "Kate, I know this is going to sound crazy," he said slowly, "but there was a reason that you bid so hard and spent so much money at that auction today. A reason beyond your own understanding."

Kate nodded and almost—but not quite—broke into a smile. "Don't give me that. I know exactly why I bid on you."

"You do?"

"Yeah, I know." She allowed herself a smile. "It was silly and petty, but it was some tangible way of proving to Beth—and myself—that I was always going to win. And I did."

Andrew shook his head. "No, that wasn't it at all," he said emphatically. "You may think it was, but—"

"I *know* why I did it, Andrew," said Kate angrily.

"Not consciously. The reason is that people who are about to die sometimes find themselves having dinner with Death."

If he had expected Kate to be shocked or surprised at his words, he was disappointed. Instead, she shrugged off what he had said, paying little attention, refusing to let it sink in. Kate was not going to be swayed. She would *not* share credit with anyone. Why should she? She had done the hard work, she had put in the long hours. She deserved every bit of recognition that was due to her.

"Well, I guess," she said, shrugging, "that's probably true if you want to get psychological. I mean, you're the death and dying counselor, and maybe I sensed that, since I'm going to die in the near future." She was silent a moment, as if thinking about what to say next, whether she should say it at all. "You know what I think about death, Andrew? Maybe it'll interest you, seeing as it's your stock-in-trade."

"It would interest me greatly."

"The first time I realized what death was, I was horrified. *Horrified*," she said. "Almost sick to my stomach."

"Why is that?" Andrew asked.

"Because I realized one day I would die, and *it would make absolutely no difference.*"

"But, Kate—"

She held up a hand, warding off his interruption. "Listen. It struck me like a punch in the stomach—the sun would still rise, people would go to work, get married, make love, quarrel, eat in great restaurants, sleep late, get fired—the world would go on, except I would not be part of it. People talk about the loss involved in death—but they're talking about the people who continue to live. The real loss is to the deceased. Dying, Andrew, is *losing*. And because we are all born to die, we all end up losers in the end."

"No, no, no, Kate. You can't look at it that way." Andrew took another stab at it, trying to make her see the danger she was in. "Kate, I know you don't believe in God. But He believes in you."

Kate tossed down her napkin and threw herself back in her chair. "Oh, come on, Andrew. Get off it! You can't honestly expect me to believe that."

Andrew had no choice but to persist. "God has sent me to be with you when you die. And if heaven is where you want to go, I'll be there to help you get there. I am an angel, Kate, and you *are* facing death—but not five years from now. Tonight, Kate." He leaned forward and put as much force behind the word as he dared. *"Tonight."*

For a moment she stared at him, horror-struck. Then her face hardened, and her eyes closed. Andrew could see that he was losing her, that her heart was shutting tight.

"You . . . are crazy," she said angrily. "And I am getting out of here—now."

She reached for her purse, but before she

could stand and leave, there was a terrible sound in the room. Norman Delmonico had risen to his feet, both of his hands at his neck. Horrible, strangled sounds were forcing themselves up through his constricted throat. It seemed that more than one person would face death that night. Mr. Norman Delmonico was fighting for his life.

Chapter Eleven

$\mathscr{M}$r. Delmonico!" Monica was the first to react to Norman's predicament. She dashed across the room. Delmonico was doubled over the table, coughing and choking.

"I saw this coming a mile away," said Tess.

Kate took charge immediately, reacting the way any doctor would in an emergency—quickly, instinctively, decisively. She grabbed Delmonico by the chin and raised his head.

"Can you breathe?" she demanded.

There was a look of terror in Delmonico's eyes as he shook his head to say no. By now the obstruction in his throat was complete. He could feel the blanket of unconsciousness stealing over him and he knew, in his soul, that death trailed in its wake. Suddenly, he realized, beyond a shadow of a doubt, that he was dying.

But Kate Calder did not allow people to die on her watch. First she grabbed the knot of his tie and yanked it loose. Then she stood behind him, bracing her hip against his lower back, and strategically placed her right fist about an inch or so above his belly button. She covered her right hand with her left, and pulled sharply and quickly in and upward.

"Come on, Norman," Kate said through clenched teeth. With surprising strength she yanked him off the floor, forcing air up through his throat. "Come on, Norman. *You're not gonna die*. Not now. Not if I can help it."

Tess was not so sure. She shot a sideways glance at Andrew. "You know anything about this, Andrew?"

"No," he said quietly. "But I'm ready for it." No matter how many times he experienced it, Andrew found it hard to watch people die. It always seemed to tear his heart from its moorings.

Norman's face grew more and more red. There was a haze in front of his eyes, and his weight was dead in Kate Calder's arms. His eyes flickered, looking at what he thought would be his last sight on earth. He saw the worry on Tess' face, the distraught look in Monica's eyes.

Then he saw Andrew, who stood in a pool of heavenly gold light. His black tuxedo was gone and in its place, he wore a dazzling white suit, his uniform as the Angel of Death. Norman Delmonico's eyes widened as he stared at Andrew, feeling his fear melt away in the calm of Andrew's smile. Kate's urgent voice hissing in his ear faded away. Suddenly all was silent and he felt a great peace pass through him, a feeling of relief, a sense of having put down a heavy burden.

Then—without warning—it all came rushing back. The lump of half-chewed veal dislodged itself from his throat and he took a huge breath, coughing and gagging as he did so. He sank down in his chair and slumped forward, gasping for breath. He closed his eyes and rubbed his temples. "Oh, my Lord," he groaned. "I can't believe it."

Kate's heart was pounding in her chest and her own breath was coming fast, an adrenaline rush screaming through her. It would take a while for her to calm down.

"Thank God," she said. "You're okay, Norman, just take slow deep breaths." She looked to Monica. "Could we have a glass of water here, please?"

Monica grabbed a glass and filled it. Norman took a small sip and then looked up at Kate and the angels. His chest was still heaving, and there were tears in his eyes.

"I'm . . . so sorry," he gasped. He looked old and worn. "I'm so terribly sorry . . ."

Kate sighed heavily. "Man, that was close. That was very, very close. Norman, you had me worried there for a minute."

Norman nodded. "I know," he wheezed. "I know . . . I could feel myself dying." His voice was unsteady and quavered wildly. "My life was coming to an end."

"Well," said Kate. "We managed to get around that one, Mr. Delmonico. You cheated death this time." She glanced over at Andrew. "Funny how that subject keeps coming up, isn't it? Death seems to be all over the place tonight."

Norman did not hear the irony in her voice. He nodded vehemently, as if agreeing with every word she said.

"Please . . . please don't laugh at me . . . ," he said. "I can't explain it, but I thought I saw the Angel of Death standing right . . ." His eyes lit on Andrew and he paled, then jumped to his feet, his chest heaving. He was terrified, but he could not take his eyes from Andrew's face. The white suit was gone—he was back in his tuxedo—but Norman knew what he had seen in those few terrifying seconds as he faced his own demise. He had seen the Angel of Death.

"You!" he said, pointing to Andrew. "It was you! You were ready for me, weren't you?"

Kate was stunned by this and looked to Andrew. But he seemed his usual calm self. He smiled at Norman.

"Yes," Andrew replied easily. "It was me. But as you can see, you're fine after all. You don't need me now, sir."

"You really should take smaller bites," said Monica, a little smile on her lips. "Chew, chew, chew. That's why God went to the trouble of inventing the incisors."

Norman looked around, fear and bewilderment showing in his eyes. "I don't know what's going on," he said, "but I'd like to leave now. I have to go."

Tess stepped up and patted him on the back, like a mother comforting a child who had just awakened from a nightmare. "I think that is a very good idea, baby," she said. "And don't worry about paying a bill. The dinner is free, on the house."

"Thank you," the elderly man gasped. Norman grabbed his coat and started for the door—then he stopped, turned back, and grabbed the wine bottle (there was still at least a glass' worth in it). *Then* he made a dash for the door.

"My goodness," said Monica, a little breathless. "I had no idea the restaurant business could be so exciting."

"Too exciting, if you want my opinion," Tess growled. "And it's hard work too."

Kate had nothing to say to any of them. She

snatched up her purse and started for the door. Andrew tried to stop her.

"Kate," he called out. "We still have to talk."

There was real fear in Kate's eyes. "No," she said. "No we don't." She turned and ran.

"Kate!" Andrew yelled, taking a step to follow her. But Tess put out a hand and stopped him.

"Let her go, baby," she said gently. "She's just not ready to hear you quite yet."

Andrew stopped and sighed, his shoulders slumped wearily. He knew that Tess was right.

Kate caught up with Norman Delmonico down Madison Avenue. The esteemed restaurant critic was waving frantically at taxis—the drivers slowed to pick him up but then sped away when they saw that their fare was a wild-eyed man clutching an open bottle of wine.

"Taxi! Taxi!" he yelled. "Oh, why don't they stop!" Delmonico managed to take a moment to calm himself and he thrust the open bottle into the pocket of his raincoat and tried again. This time a taxi cruised to a halt. But Kate could not let him get away. She *had* to speak to him. She had to find out exactly what he had seen. She picked up the hem of her long gown and ran after him as fast as her high heels would allow.

"Mr. Delmonico!" Kate called. "Wait!"

Norman was half in the cab when he saw her. He hesitated a moment, then turned back to face her.

"Are . . . are you one, too?" His voice wavered and she could see that he was still terrified. Norman Delmonico would never be the same again. He had looked into the face of an angel and somehow, he felt he had been in the very presence of God.

"No, no," she said quickly. "I'm not . . . no." Kate was almost as agitated as Delmonico, her words spilling out. "Please, please tell me. What did you see? What happened up there?"

Delmonico took a deep breath. "You were there," he said. "You saw what was happening.

I almost died. You saved my life. But he . . . *he* was waiting for me."

Kate grabbed Norman by the shoulders. "Andrew?"

"Yes."

"The man in the tuxedo?"

Delmonico nodded and swallowed hard. "Yes . . . yes, but he wasn't wearing that anymore. He was wearing . . . I don't know how to explain it. He was wearing clothes, but more . . . *real*. He had hair and hands and a face, but they were more . . . they were *more*." Delmonico strained to put into words just what he had seen. "It was as if for all my life I'd been looking at nothing more than a reflection of the world and then suddenly I *saw*—I really saw what the world was made of—I'm sorry. I just can't explain it."

He did not have the words to explain it, but Kate did. She knew exactly what the old man was trying to convey, and now she knew that all Andrew had said was true. She could hardly believe it, but she knew in the deepest part of her that there was no way now that she could bring herself to deny it.

"You saw the ultimate reality," she said, but it was as if she were talking to herself.

"Yes! Yes, that's it," said Delmonico. "That's it exactly. Tell me, please, what were you talking about? What did the angel tell you? You must tell me."

"Then he *is* an angel," Kate said, looking up at the building as if expecting to see Andrew up there in the dark windows.

"Yes!" Delmonico almost yelped. "It's incredible. It's terrifying. But it's wonderful too! But what did he tell you?"

"He told me—" Suddenly her voice was tight and blocked by hot tears. "He told me that I'm going to die tonight."

The words hit Delmonico like a slap and he recoiled, staggering back a few steps, the look on his face a mixture of awe and terror. Kate turned away and walked back toward the building, the blinding reality of her situation pulsing through her brain. Suddenly she realized that her life depended on what she had just left behind.

The "Chez Tess" plaque was gone and, with a rising panic, she discovered that the tall glass double doors of the office block were locked tight. Overcome with dread and alarm, she surrendered to the hysteria resonating within her. Terrible wracking sobs rose up and shook her and she pounded on the door, desperate to get back inside.

"Open the door! Please!" The words had to force themselves out, pushing through her cries, but the doors were unyielding. Anguish overcame her like a great, dark cloud and she sank to her knees on the cold stone floor, sobbing wretchedly in the doorway, alone in the night.

Chapter Twelve

*T*here was only one place Kate could go.

Her home—two bare, rather antiseptic rooms in a nondescript apartment building in the East 30s—held no attraction for her. It was nothing more than a place where she slept, changed her clothes, and ordered takeout meals for one. Her true home, the place where she felt comfortable, was the laboratory at Nichols BioTech. So it was there she went, returning to her place in the world like a homing pigeon.

Of course, at that hour, the lab was empty and dark, the most dedicated of the researchers having called it a night many hours before. In

fact, on an ordinary night, a night less important than this one, Kate herself would probably
have been the last to leave.

She was glad that the place was empty, because
she was still distraught and terrified, and the
last thing she wanted was to be seen in such a
state. Her hands were trembling as she unlocked
the door to the building, and it was all she could
do to punch her code number into the alarm
plate just inside the front door. She swept down
the familiar hallways, running for the lab, the
click of her high heels loud and eerie in the
empty space.

Kate was going to her research the way a certain type of believer seeks out a Bible. It was
something to hold close, something to have faith
in—something that just might be able to save
her. Kate had never before been so frightened—
not of dying. She had never been afraid of dying.
Now she found herself terrified by the notion of
the unknown. She needed the safety and security of *knowledge* to save her. And yet finding herself in her beloved laboratory did not bring the
comfort she had hoped for.

She had completely forgotten about the safe. It had been installed that day, really just a few hours before—but it was a day that already seemed to be part of a very distant past. Kate could not believe that so much had changed in such a short time. Her life, her beliefs, had been shaken to the very roots by a series of events she could never have foreseen. No one—no mortal being— could have guessed what the Books and Bachelors Luncheon and the auction would set in motion. Before that night, Kate Calder had never thought for a moment about the possibility of the existence of angels. Now she was surrounded by them.

Kate snapped on the desk lamp and swiveled the arm until it hung precariously over the edge of the counter. The light shone on the safe, the LED code glowing red in the semidarkness: "System Locked." She knelt at the safe and began to punch in her access number—but in that moment the desk lamp toppled over, crashing to the floor. Kate screamed and jumped back, accidentally hitting the panel of buttons on the lock pad, scrambling the numbers. Instantly the red LED readout changed, flashing "System Frozen," followed by the message: "Begin 12 hr sequence." Numbers began ticking a second at a time, moving backward from 12:00.

For a moment, Kate could not quite comprehend what had happened, staring in shock at the numbers and the message.

"No, no, no, *no!*" Kate's voice ran the scale from a moan to a scream as she desperately began hitting the keypad, frantically trying to override the system and enter the correct code. Like a mother cut off from an infant child, she *ached* to get at her papers. They were the only things, she thought, that could keep her whole and sane through the rest of the dark night.

But the system she had insisted on worked too well. She pounded the safe angrily, furious at this stupid, inanimate object—but also angry at herself, angry at her stupidity and her overweening pride. Slumping to the floor, her head in her hands, she fought her tears for as long as she could but, inevitably, surrendered to them.

"Oh, God," she sobbed. "I don't want to die. Help me. *Please* . . . Oh, God, help me . . ."

"Don't be afraid," said Andrew softly.

Kate turned and saw Andrew standing in the doorway. The tuxedo was gone, replaced by his white suit. In the dim light of the room he was glowing, shining with a brilliant light, filling the once dim room with God's love.

Kate felt her throat go dry, and for a moment it was difficult for her to find the words to say. "You *are* the angel," she said, "the Angel of Death, aren't you?"

Andrew nodded. "Yes, I am."

Kate knew what she was feeling in that moment. Andrew's sudden appearance had swept away the panic and the fear that had threatened to overwhelm her. In its place she felt a strange calm sweep through her. She could feel the peace deep inside her. She looked at him for a long moment, then sat down on the floor and laughed— and she knew that she was laughing at herself.

"Funny," she said. "It's really funny . . . I studied all the textbooks, read all the journals, and I always had some strange peace thinking I at least knew what disease I would die from and, more or less, when I would go." She shook her head, amazed that she could have been so positive about something over which she had no control. "I never counted on an accident, something random coming along to interrupt my carefully planned calendar. An accident . . . is that how it's going to happen, Andrew?"

Very slowly, Andrew got down on his knees, his face level with Kate's. "I don't know exactly how or when, Kate," he said gently. "But I do know this: that when it happens, I'll be there . . . Kate, I don't want to scare you, but if I've been sent here to show you the way home, then there's a reason. And that reason is usually death."

Kate studied his face for a moment and then realized that there was only one thing to do.

"So," she said with a shrug, "we wait."

"On the other hand, death could come very close to you and pass you by. It happens all the time . . ."

Kate closed her eyes and shook her head. "Andrew, please don't try to make me feel better. I understand now. I see you as clearly as Norman Delmonico did. The Angel of Death . . ." She laughed her hollow, mirthless laugh. "The Angel of Death comes for one reason."

"Really?" Andrew replied, raising an eyebrow. "Norman Delmonico is still alive, isn't he?"

Kate thought for a moment. "Yes, but—"

"No buts, Kate," he said, interrupting. "He's a little shaken up, maybe he's learned something. Maybe he won't be rude to waiters in the next restaurant he reviews. But he's still alive. I was there to help him had it been his time. But it wasn't. Death comes close, but sometimes it does not claim you."

"Oh, Andrew," Kate said. She didn't know whether or not to allow herself a moment of hope or to surrender completely to despair. There were tears in her eyes.

Andrew did his best to explain. "It's like this. A man who's been in a bar drinking may or may not run a red light later on. A woman who stops to read a magazine in a supermarket misses driv-ing through that very intersection by just a few seconds. Those are the 'what-ifs' and the 'if onlys' that we don't see until the next morning."

"But you said I bid on you for a reason."

"And you did. So you could be guided to where you had to go. Tonight you were where you were supposed to be. You had to be there to save the life of Norman Delmonico. God sees the moments because, where He is, those moments have already happened. God knows what your tomorrow looks like, Kate, because He's already there. Yesterday, today, and tomorrow—He holds them all in His hand, all at once. And He holds you there too."

A small smile flickered across Kate's lips. "So, it comes down to what I said before . . . We wait."

Andrew smiled back. "We wait."

Wearily, Kate got to her feet, righted the fallen desk lamp, then walked across the room to a small refrigerator. She opened the door and pulled out a bottle of Perrier Jouet "Fleur de Champagne," a twin of the bottle they had shared at dinner.

"I'm surprised that wasn't in the safe as well," said Andrew.

Kate laughed a little. "Couldn't keep it nice and cold in the safe, Andrew. And I knew there was no point keeping it at home, because I knew there would be nothing to celebrate at home. Anything wonderful that was going to happen to me was going to happen here."

She unwrapped the thick gold foil, pulled off the wire cage, and popped the cork. "And now you know what I was saving it for," she said. "But in my wildest dreams, I didn't think I would be sharing it with you, Andrew."

"Who would you have shared it with?" Andrew asked. "I mean, you couldn't stand in the middle of the lab and drink the whole bottle, could you?"

Kate smiled. "No, I was going to share it with everybody. The day I cracked the code I was going to be nice to everybody. They wouldn't have recognized me—Dr. Kate Calder, little Miss Sweetness and Light. Just for a day."

"Maybe you should have started sooner."

"Maybe I should have. But it's too late now."

There were no elegant glass flutes for this bottle of champagne; instead Kate grabbed a couple of glass beakers from the counter, checked quickly to see that there were no noxious chemicals within, then slopped some of the champagne in. She handed one to Andrew.

"You know," said Andrew, "there are a lot of people who aren't given an opportunity like this."

"What opportunity would that be?" Kate asked.

"They never get a chance to say good-bye."

Kate half smiled. "I was an orphan," she said. "I don't *have* anybody to say good-bye to. I grew up with thirty-two other kids in a great big, red brick building maintained by the state. I'll bet you can guess how much fun that was."

"Ah," said Andrew, as if that explained everything. "It's no wonder you don't like to share."

She nodded and sipped her champagne. "Yeah . . . maybe. I never had anything that was new. Or anything that was really mine." She could not help herself—she glanced over at the safe containing her precious breakthrough research. "At least," she added, "not until now."

Andrew followed the line of her gaze. He looked at the safe for a moment. "Oh, Kate," he said. "That's not yours. It doesn't belong to you."

"Not mine?" said Kate. She looked at him and blinked a couple of times. "What do you mean, not mine, Andrew? It's mine. It's mine because I found it."

Andrew nodded. "That's right, you *found* it. That discovery isn't yours any more than the North Pole belonged to Admiral Peary or the ocean belonged to Jacques Cousteau. The wonders of the universe, the physics and the thermodynamics, the medicines that are being found in the rain forest, the gene sequence in your precious chromosome—those belong to God, not you. The miracle is not that you found some scientific breakthrough, Kate. The miracle is that God put it there to be found and that the person who found it happened to be you. And there is a reason it was you, Kate."

"That's one way of looking at it," said Kate as she poured herself some more of the champagne. "It sort of takes the wind out of my sails, though. Thanks a lot, Andrew."

Andrew shook his head quickly. The miracle

is that God chose to reveal it through *you*. He trusted *you* with it. And you've locked it up. The way you've locked up your heart: so safe, so secure, so guarded that now even you can't get into it."

Kate felt something deep within her move, and tears came to her eyes, but they weren't tears of anger or self-pity. "I . . . was starting to believe during these last few years."

"Believe?" Andrew asked.

Kate nodded. "That's right, I started to accept the possibility of the existence of God . . . The more work I did in science, the more I became awed by the staggering complexity of this world—and I started to think that the odds of it all coming together so perfectly simply by accident—" Kate shrugged and took another gulp of her champagne "—that the idea of perfect *randomness* seemed harder to accept than the possibility that it had all been designed that way. Designed by . . . a really Great Designer. And if that was true, then I felt very, very small. And meaningless. And to get the attention of somebody like that, well . . . I figured I had to do something that mattered."

"And you did, Kate," said Andrew. "You started to believe. Belief is the foundation of faith. And once you've got that, you have started on your way to knowing God."

Kate raised her beaker of champagne in a mocking little toast. "Yeah. But too late."

"No," said Andrew. "It is *never* too late. God loves you, Kate, and He trusted you with something special. Now, will you trust Him?"

Instantly, Kate knew what Andrew was talking about. "That's it, isn't it? He wants me to do the one thing I can't do." She tried to keep the tears from her voice. "I can't do it, Andrew. It's too hard. I've worked too long at this to give it away. Maybe it's not mine—but it certainly doesn't belong to anybody else."

"You have to be willing to share the glory, Kate," Andrew countered. "Maybe even risk that Beth and all the others working here take it, take it all. It doesn't matter, because the information inside that safe is more important than who found it first; it's more important than any fame or glory."

Kate spoke deliberately and slowly. "If I hand over the combination of that safe to Beth, and she gets hold of my research, I might as well die anyway, because I won't have anything left to live for."

"But think of all the people who will live instead," said Andrew. "You will have given them life—they might not know it. But you'll know and God will know."

The impact of Andrew's words was profound, and for a moment her head reeled with the thought. She had spent so much time trying to protect her precious work that the idea of giving it away—at the behest of God, no less—was mind-boggling. But after all she had seen, heard, experienced that night, it made sense. She was silent for a long time as she thought it over.

Then she whispered, "Okay . . . okay . . . I will share my research with Beth." She was silent for a moment. "But will I live until she comes in for work tomorrow morning?"

Andrew shrugged. "I cannot say . . . I just don't know."

"Then it has to be tonight," said Kate firmly. "There's no time left, is there?"

Chapter Thirteen

$\mathcal{C}$hez Tess had ceased to exist.

Only moments after Kate left the restaurant, Monica, Tess, and Adam had gotten busy striking the set. It did not take long to reduce the elegant restaurant to the rubbish-strewn mess it had been earlier that afternoon. Cardboard boxes and other debris now stood where there had been a kitchen, a dining room, a bar, and a dance floor. The baby grand piano was long gone, as was the beautiful commercial range and all the other kitchen equipment.

Adam rolled a big, wooden cable spool into

the middle of the room. "Where does this go?" he asked.

"Oh, just set it down right there," Tess ordered. Adam did as he was told, then sat down on the spool and fished a drumstick out of his suit pocket and began eating, gnawing with obvious relish.

Tess looked at him as he ate. "What are you doing?" she asked. "What is that you've got there, Adam?"

"It's some of your leftover pheasant," he replied. "It's really great stuff, Tess. Excellent."

"Yeah, well," Tess replied, sounding a little disappointed. "There's plenty of pheasant left over. Kate had veal, if you recall—and Andrew went right along with it. He had veal too."

Adam stopped eating abruptly. "You mean Beth," he said. "Beth, right?"

Monica and Tess stared at him for a moment.

"Who's Beth?" Monica asked.

"Yes," said Tess. "Who on earth is Beth? Kate was Andrew's assignment."

"*Who's Beth*?" Adam jumped to his feet. "Beth

was the doctor, the one at the auction. Beth is the woman you just did all this for."

Monica looked genuinely alarmed. "Adam! Andrew had dinner with a woman named Kate. Her name is Kate. Kate Calder."

"I don't understand," said Adam. "Who is this Kate Calder? Where did she come from all of a sudden?"

"*She's* the doctor from the auction." Then it dawned on Monica. There had been a horrible mix-up. "She's the doctor who *won* the auction."

Monica looked at Tess. Tess shook her head. "Uh-oh . . ." She turned to Adam. "You better get going. Find Andrew and figure this whole thing out." Tess nodded to herself. This was exactly the kind of thing she had been concerned about—right at the very beginning she had felt uncertain about this assignment.

"I'm on my way," said Adam. After he left, Tess said a prayer and asked God to turn around the situation if needed.

It was just after three in the morning when Kate's car rolled to a stop in front of Beth's house. There were lights burning, and there was the intermittent light of a television, flashing shadows on the ceiling and walls. It surprised Kate that Beth would be such a night owl, but it would make her task a little easier. Kate took a deep breath.

"Well, so far, so good," she said.

"You okay?" Andrew asked.

Kate nodded. "Let's just hope I don't trip on the way to the door and fracture my skull," she said with a little smile. The two of them got out of the car, but Andrew hung back, letting Kate go up to the house by herself. As she went, Andrew looked down the street and saw Adam walking purposefully toward him. Andrew had no doubt that Adam's sudden appearance did not bode well for someone. Concerned, he looked back to Kate.

Kate managed to get to the front door of Beth's small house without serious injury. She rang the doorbell and waited . . . and waited. Impatient, she rang again and heard nothing from inside the house, no sound of footsteps, nothing—except the murmur of the television. She walked to a window and peered inside.

Beth was lying on the couch, dressed in her nightgown and bathrobe. She appeared to be sound asleep. Kate rapped on the window with her knuckles. "Beth! Beth!" she called. "Wake up!"

But Beth did not stir. Kate suddenly felt alarmed. She pounded on the window a little harder. "*Beth!*" Kate was yelling now. "Wake up!"

Then Kate looked down and saw something that frightened her terribly. Lying on the living room rug was a large, furry dog—and dogs did *not* sleep through the kind of racket she had been making. In an instant, she knew what was going on, and she did not hesitate. She grabbed a flowerpot full of geraniums and hurled it through the window, shattering it. Then she turned. "Andrew! I need help!"

But both Andrew and Adam had vanished. It was up to Kate Calder to save Beth's life all on her own.

An hour later, Beth was in the hospital, and Kate was talking to the attending physician. It was the dead of night, and the hospital was quiet—Beth had been taken into the emergency room.

"People get poisoned from those old heaters all the time, and nobody seems to catch it before it's too late," the doctor told Kate. "How did you know it was carbon monoxide?"

"I saw the dog through the window," Kate replied. "And they don't sleep through doorbells."

"Well, it's a miracle you were there," the doctor said. "If you hadn't been, she would have died tonight."

Those words hit Kate hard. She stood still in the middle of the hospital corridor and let the words sink in. Twice in one night she had prevented a death. Andrew's words were coming true.

"Are you all right?" the doctor asked.

Kate smiled—she almost laughed out loud. "Yes, I am," she said. "I think I'm fine! Can I see her?"

"If she's awake—why don't you go and find out? She's in 403—right down the hall."

"Thank you," Kate said. It was a short walk down the bare hospital corridor, but in those few yards, Kate's life underwent a profound change. She had made up her mind what to do.

Beth was still a little groggy from the hours she had spent in the room filled with carbon monoxide, but the oxygen tube inserted in her nose was uncomfortable, and would not allow her to sleep. She was pale and weak, but she smiled when Kate entered her room.

"Still here?" she asked.

Kate nodded. "I was just talking to your doctor. You're only going to be here overnight."

"What about Bruno?" Beth asked.

"He'll be fine."

Beth stirred a little under the covers. "It's very scary," she said. "All I remember is getting really, really sleepy."

"That's how it happens," Kate replied. "You don't see it or smell it. You just go to sleep and you never wake up." It sounded to Kate like an ideal way to die.

"If you hadn't been there . . ." Beth shook her head slowly. "And what *were* you doing at my house at three o'clock in the morning?"

"I . . . uh . . ." Kate shrugged and laughed. "I don't know. I have no idea. Look, Beth, get some sleep." She stood to go, then stopped. The reluctance to share her discovery and the credit for finding it—once upon a time a reflex almost built into her genetic makeup—had suddenly vanished. It was foolish for her to have come so far, to have learned so much, without going through with the plan; the plan that Andrew had taught her had come from God. Kate sat down again.

"I do know why I was there, Beth. I came to your house . . ." This was it. She took a deep breath. "I came to tell you that I had found a gene sequence, Beth. I'm almost there."

Beth, her head on the pillow, nodded slightly. "I see," she said. "Well, congratulations."

"I was thinking, maybe if we worked . . . together . . . we'd get there sooner. That is if . . . you want to work with me."

Kate Calder had been so myopic, so wrapped up in her own cares and obsessions, that it had never occurred to her that Beth might *not want* to have anything to do with her. Of course, Kate could hardly have blamed her if that was the way she felt. Not a day had passed in the last year or two that Kate hadn't made some nasty crack or cutting remark to Beth. Kate could only look back at her own bad behavior with horror. She had been so insensitive and uncaring . . . She was going to try to change. And she hoped that there was really such a thing as forgiveness.

Beth smiled at her. "This isn't like you at all, Kate. What's happened to you all of a sudden?"

Kate smiled brightly. "I discovered something else," she said. "You can do wonderful things, if you don't care who gets the credit."

"That's quite a change of heart," Beth said. Then she noticed that Kate was still dressed in the red velvet evening gown that she had worn to the restaurant. "How was your date, by the way?"

"Fascinating," Kate replied.

Kate walked out of the hospital and into the sights and soft sounds of the dawn of a new day. There was a light, fresh-smelling breeze blowing and the sky was clear except for some thin, pinkish clouds. There was birdsong in the air. All in all it promised to be a fine day. Kate filled her lungs with the sweet air as if breathing in hope. Andrew was waiting for her in the parking lot of the hospital, and she crossed the street, walking toward him. He could tell by the way she walked that there was something different about this Kate Calder, that she had become a new person. There was a serenity about her and a confidence in her step that had not been there before.

She walked up to him and looked him in the eye for a moment before speaking. "I understand it now," she said, nodding to herself. "It was Beth who would have died last night and not me, after all."

Andrew smiled softly and nodded. He shrugged as if apologizing for something. "Yes, she was supposed to win the auction, not you. I was supposed to take her to dinner, but I never knew her name, so when you ended up winning . . ." He shrugged again. "You can imagine what I thought . . . particularly when you told me about your illness, back there at the restaurant."

"You thought it was me," Kate said. "You thought that I was the one who was going to die."

"That's right. I thought it was you."

Kate glanced back at the hospital. "I guess that's why Beth wanted to win so bad. Somehow she saw you coming, and I—as usual—had to get there first. The old me, that is." And she meant that. The old Kate was really gone—and gone for good. She could feel it, as if a part of her—a malignant part—had been cut out of her. And although she had not had a wink of sleep and had been through a harrowing night, she felt relaxed and refreshed.

"I'm sorry," said Andrew. "I'm sorry that you had to go through it. It could not have been easy for you."

"Hey," said Kate, laughing out loud. "God made a mistake. Surely this isn't the first time He's done it."

"No," Andrew replied quickly. "*People* make mistakes. Sometimes even *angels* make mistakes."

Andrew gazed at her for a moment, and his voice lowered. "But God doesn't make mistakes. He saved two lives last night instead of one. Three counting Norman Delmonico. I told you that death sometimes passes you by. God chose to make it pass by last night, and that was His decision. We cannot know why. But we know the result. He saved your life in one way and saved Beth's in another."

"Yes," Kate said, "I think maybe He did. So, I've still got a few more years left, huh?"

Andrew nodded. "Yes, you do, Kate. And now you know what to do with them, right?"

Kate nodded. "I do know now. Thanks to

you." She shook her head slowly. "It was certainly a wild way of finding out, I'll have to say that. Do you always operate like this?"

"We work the way God wants us to," Andrew replied. "It's really very simple."

Kate sighed. "A heck of a way to earn a living," she said with a little smile. "Can I ask you one more question?"

"Of course," said Andrew. "Ask me anything."

"These few years that I have left—" she paused a moment as she thought calmly about the end of her life. "—when those years are over—"

"When they're over, Kate . . ." He took her hand and kissed it gently. "Then I'll see you for dinner . . ."